**BUCKET OF TALES**

# Love In
# The Shadows
# Of Fear

BY

**Pugal** *Yazhini*

**To be Continued**

# Preface of

## *Love in The Shadows of Fear*

L ove, heists, and mysteries three captivating
genres that have captivated readers for
centuries. In this single **BOOK**, we explore the
different themes and characters that make
these genres so enthralling. From the depths of
love to the thrill of the perfect heist, and the
mystery of an unsolved crime, this book takes
us on a journey through the world of fiction,
reminding us of the endless possibilities that
await within the pages of a good book.

With *Love* & **Fear**,
  *[* **Pugal** *Yazhini ]*

**To be Continued**

# Contents

## Suspense & Thriller 115

# Love In
# The Shadows
# Of Fear

# Love & Romance

# Colors of Love an Urban Tale

## Chapter 1

Pugal was a young man living in the heart of the city. He loved the hustle and bustle of urban life, the endless possibilities and the ever-changing landscape. But amidst the chaos, he found himself feeling a little lost and alone.

That was until he met Yazhini. She was a beautiful, talented artist who captured his heart from the moment they met. They shared a love for the city, but more than that, they shared a deep connection that seemed to transcend time and space.

Their love blossomed amidst the concrete and steel of the city, with Pugal showing Yazhini all his favourite spots and introducing her to the unique flavour of the urban culture. They spent countless hours exploring the city, discovering hidden gems and creating new memories together.

But their love was not without its challenges. Pugal was a dreamer, always chasing the next big thing, while Yazhini was more grounded and practical. They struggled to find common ground, with each feeling like they were constantly compromising.

Their relationship was put to the test when Pugal was offered a once-in-a-lifetime opportunity to pursue his dreams.

It would mean leaving the city and Yazhini behind, but it was a chance he couldn't pass up. Yazhini was torn between supporting Pugal's dreams and staying true to herself.

She loved Pugal deeply but couldn't see herself leaving the city that had become her home.

As the days ticked by, Pugal and Yazhini struggled to find a solution that would work for both of them. But in the end, they realized that their love was worth fighting for.

They found a way to make it work, with Pugal pursuing his dreams while still keeping a connection with Yazhini and the city they both loved.

Their love story may have been unconventional, but it was real and true. And in a world that often feels cold and disconnected, Pugal and Yazhini's love shone like a bright light, illuminating the beauty of urban culture and the power of love.

# **Chapter 2**

Pugal pursued his dreams, he found success and recognition beyond his wildest dreams. He travelled the world, meeting new people and experiencing new cultures.

But no matter where he went, his heart always remained with Yazhini and the city they called home. Yazhini, meanwhile, continued to create and showcase her art, drawing inspiration from the urban landscape that surrounded her.

She found new ways to express herself and discovered a sense of purpose that she had never felt before. Despite the distance and the challenges, their love continued to grow stronger. They made a conscious effort to stay connected, calling and texting each other regularly, and visiting each other whenever possible.

And then, one day, Pugal came home. He had achieved everything he had set out to do, but he realized that none of it mattered without Yazhini by his side.

He found Yazhini where he had left her, in the heart of the city, surrounded by the art and culture they both loved. He got down on one knee and proposed to her, promising to love her and cherish her always.

Yazhini was overjoyed and accepted his proposal with tears in her eyes. They embraced, knowing that they had overcome so much to be together. And as they looked out over the city that had brought them together, they knew that their love was something special, something that would never fade or diminish.

They were each other's home, and no matter where life took them, they would always find their way back to each other.

# **Chapter 3**

In the following years, Pugal and Yazhini built a life together, filled with love, laughter, and a shared appreciation for the urban culture that had brought them together. They continued to explore the city, finding new and exciting art installations, street performances, and cultural events.

They even started their own creative venture, combining Pugal's business acumen with Yazhini's artistic vision to launch a successful boutique shop that showcased the work of local artists.

Their love only grew stronger with each passing day, and they knew that they were meant to be together forever.

But then, a sudden tragedy struck. Pugal was diagnosed with a life-threatening illness, and his doctors told him that he only had a few months left to live. Devastated but determined, Pugal decided to spend his remaining time doing what he loved most: exploring the city with Yazhini by his side. They visited all their favourite spots, discovering new hidden gems and re-living cherished memories.

They spent long nights talking about their hopes and dreams, reminiscing about the past, and making the most of the precious time they had left. As Pugal's condition worsened, they knew that the end was near. But even in his final moments, Pugal remained grateful for the life he had lived and the love he had shared with Yazhini.

And when he passed away, surrounded by the art and culture that had defined their relationship, Yazhini knew that his love would live on forever.

She continued to explore the city they had loved together, finding comfort and solace in the memories they had created and the love they had shared. And even as the years passed, she knew that Pugal's spirit would always be with her, guiding her on her journey and reminding her of the power of love and urban culture.

## **Chapter 4**

In the years that followed, Yazhini continued to horon Pugal's memory, both in her personal and professional life. She expanded their boutique shop, showcasing even more local artists and helping to promote urban culture in the city.

But despite her success, Yazhini never forgot the love that she and Pugal had shared. And so, she decided to create a lasting tribute to their relationship and their passion for urban culture.

She commissioned a muralist to create a large-scale artwork in the heart of the city, depicting the vibrant colors and dynamic energy that had always inspired her and Pugal. The mural featured images of the city's iconic landmarks, as well as subtle nods to the love story that had begun on its streets.

The mural quickly became a beloved landmark in the city, drawing crowds from all over to admire its beauty and reflect on the power of love and urban culture. And for Yazhini, it was a symbol of the enduring love she shared with Pugal, a reminder of the joy and inspiration he had brought into her life, and a tribute to the city that had brought them together.

As she looked out over the mural, Yazhini knew that her love story with Pugal had been a rare and beautiful thing, a testament to the power of following your dreams and embracing the unique beauty of the world around you.

And she knew that wherever life took her next, she would always carry his memory with her, inspired by his unwavering spirit and the love that had changed her life forever.

## **Chapter 5**

The story of Pugal and Yazhini is one of love, inspiration, and the power of urban culture to bring people together. And despite the challenges they faced, their love ultimately prevailed, creating a lasting legacy that would continue to inspire generations to come.

As Yazhini looked out over the vibrant, bustling city that had brought her and Pugal together, she knew that their love story was far from over. She could feel his presence all around her, guiding her on her journey and reminding her of the joy and beauty of life.

And she knew that no matter what challenges lay ahead, she would always carry his memory with her, inspired by his spirit and the love that had changed her life forever. With a smile on her face, Yazhini took Pugal's hand and looked out over the city they had loved together. And together, they knew that their love would continue to shine, illuminating the world around them with its unique and enduring beauty.

# Perilous Journey

In the kingdom of Eldrid, there lived a beautiful princess named Elara. She had long, curly hair the colors of chestnuts and bright green eyes that shone like emeralds. She was kind and intelligent, and loved to spend her days exploring the castle gardens and reading books in the library.

One day, while wandering in the gardens, she met a handsome knight named Tristan. He was tall and muscular, with blonde hair and blue eyes that sparkled in the sunlight. They immediately felt a strong connection, and over time, they fell deeply in love.

However, their happiness was short-lived. The king, Elara's father, disapproved of Tristan and forbade him from seeing his daughter.

The king had chosen another suitor for Elara, a wealthy prince from a neighbouring kingdom who would bring political alliances and prosperity to Eldrid. Despite their love for each other, Elara and Tristan knew they could never be together.

Tristan was heartbroken, and decided to leave Eldrid and travel to distant lands in search of adventure and meaning.

Years passed, and Elara became queen after her father's death. She ruled with grace and kindness, but deep down, she never forgot her love for Tristan.

One day, a young knight named Marcus arrived at the castle with news of a great quest. He told her of a magical crystal that had the power to grant any wish, and that it was hidden in a distant land.

Elara knew what she had to do. She gathered a group of knights and set out on a perilous journey to find the crystal. After months of travel and many battles, they finally reached the cave where the crystal was hidden.

They fought their way through fierce monsters and treacherous traps, and finally, they found the crystal. With the crystal in hand, Elara made her wish-to be reunited with Tristan, the love of her life. And just like that, he appeared before her, standing tall and strong, his blue eyes shining with joy and love.

They fell into each other's arms, tears streaming down their faces. They knew that they had been apart for too long, but their love had only grown stronger over time. They returned to Eldrid together, where they were married in a grand ceremony.

As they ruled the kingdom side by side, they faced many challenges, but they did so with love and understanding. They knew that the crystal had granted their wish, but it was their own love and determination that had brought them together.

And so, Elara and Tristan lived happily ever after, ruling their kingdom with compassion and wisdom, and proving that true love can conquer all.

# Quest for Parenthood

In the year 2125, the world had changed. Gone were the days of war, famine, and disease. People had finally come together to create a utopian society where everyone had access to basic needs and education, and where love was celebrated in all its forms.

In this world, there lived a young woman named Maya. She was kind and compassionate, with long brown hair and hazel eyes that sparkled with intelligence. She worked as a teacher, helping children learn and grow, and she was loved by all who knew her.

One day, as she was walking in the park, she met a man named Alex. He was tall and handsome, with dark hair and piercing blue eyes. They struck up a conversation, and over time, they fell deeply in love.

They spent their days exploring the city, talking about their hopes and dreams, and enjoying each other's company. They were happy, but they both knew that something was missing. They longed to have a child, to bring new life into the world and share their love with another being.

In this utopian society, however, having a child was not a simple matter. There were strict regulations in place to ensure that all children were born into families who could provide them with the best possible life. Maya and Alex knew that they would have to go through a rigorous screening process, and even then, there was no guarantee that they would be approved.

They decided to try anyway. They went through the screening process, which included interviews, genetic testing, and psychological evaluations. They passed with flying colors, and were finally given permission to have a child.

Nine months later, Maya gave birth to a beautiful baby girl. They named her Ava, and they loved her with all their hearts. They raised her in a world where love and compassion were the norm, and she grew up to be a kind and intelligent young woman, just like her mother. As Ava grew older, Maya and Alex knew that it was time to let her go out into the world and find her own path.

They knew that they had given her the best possible start in life, and they were proud of the person she had become.

And so, as Maya and Alex watched their daughter leave the nest, they knew that their love had created something beautiful and lasting. They knew that their utopian society had given them the opportunity to create a family and a legacy of love, and they felt grateful for the chance to be a part of it. But what lay ahead for Maya and Alex, and for their society as a whole, was uncertain.

They knew that there were still challenges to be faced, and that their world was not perfect. But they also knew that as long as love was at the heart of everything they did, they would be able to overcome any obstacle and create a better future for themselves and for their children.

# The Medical term of Love

Dr. Alexander Thompson was one of the most respected cardiac surgeons in the world, with a reputation for saving the lives of patients who had been given up on by others.

His knowledge of the human heart was unmatched, and he had made countless breakthroughs in the field of cardiology. But when he met Emily, he knew that he was facing his greatest challenge yet.

Emily was a beautiful young woman with a rare and complex heart condition that had left her struggling to breathe and in constant pain. She had been referred to Dr. Thompson by her cardiologist, who had heard of his expertise in the field of heart transplants.

Emily knew that she was facing an uphill battle, but she had faith that Dr. Thompson could save her life.

Dr. Thompson was immediately struck by Emily's beauty and her determination to fight for her life. He knew that she was special, and he felt a connection to her that he couldn't explain.

As he began to examine her medical records and test results, he realized that her condition was even more serious than he had anticipated.

Emily's heart was failing rapidly, and she was in urgent need of a transplant. But finding a suitable donor was proving to be a challenge, and Dr. Thompson knew that time was running out. He made the difficult decision to put Emily on a waiting list for a donor heart, but he also began to explore other options.

As he worked tirelessly to find a solution, Dr. Thompson found himself drawn to Emily in a way that he had never experienced before. He found himself thinking about her constantly, and he couldn't shake the feeling that there was something special about her.

Meanwhile, Emily's condition continued to deteriorate, and she found herself struggling to stay alive. But even as she fought for her life, she couldn't shake the feeling that there was something different about Dr. Thompson.

She felt a connection to him that she couldn't explain, and she found herself drawn to him in a way that she couldn't understand.

As the days turned into weeks, Dr. Thompson and his team of researchers continued to work tirelessly to find a solution for Emily's condition. And finally, they found it.

Dr. Thompson had discovered a ground-breaking new treatment that could save Emily's life. The treatment involved using stem cells to repair the damaged tissue in her heart, and it was a risky procedure that had never been tried before.

But Dr. Thompson was determined to save Emily's life, and he knew that the treatment was her best hope for survival. As he began the procedure, he felt a sense of hope and determination that he had never experienced before.

The procedure was a success, and Emily's heart was stronger than ever before. She was free from the pain and suffering that had plagued her for years, and she knew that she had Dr. Thompson to thank for her new lease on life.

As Emily and Dr. Thompson spent more time together, they began to realize that their connection was more than just a professional one.

They had fallen in love, and they knew that they wanted to spend the rest of their lives together.

In the end, Emily and Dr. Thompson got married, and they continued to work together to help patients with heart conditions.

They knew that they had been brought together for a reason, and they were grateful for the love and happiness that they had found together.

# A Love That Endures

Alex is a studious young man, always buried in his textbooks and focused on his studies. Samantha, on the other hand, is a free spirit, with a love for adventure and a zest for life.

One day, Alex was sitting in the library, poring over his notes, when Samantha walked by. She was humming to herself, lost in thought, when she caught Alex's eye. He couldn't help but smile at her, and to his surprise, she smiled back.

He watched as she made her way across the room, weaving through the maze of bookshelves until she was standing right in front of him.

"Hi," she said, flashing him a smile. "I'm Samantha. Mind if I sit down?"

Alex was caught off guard, but he quickly recovered, nodding his head and gesturing for her to take a seat.

They started talking, and before they knew it, the hours had flown by. They talked about everything, from their favourite books to their hopes and dreams for the future.

And as the sun began to set outside, Alex realized that he had never felt more alive. With Samantha by his side, he felt like anything was possible, like the world was full of infinite possibilities.

And so, that chance encounter in the library would change their lives forever, setting them on a path that would lead to great love and heartbreak, but also to a deeper understanding of what it means to truly live.

As the weeks went by, they became inseparable. They spent every moment they could together, exploring the city, trying new foods, and making memories that would last a lifetime.

But just as they were settling into their new life together, Alex got sick. It started with a cough that wouldn't go away, but soon he was in the hospital, hooked up to machines and fighting for his life.

Samantha refused to leave his side, holding his hand and whispering words of love and encouragement as he struggled to get better. But as the days turned into weeks, it became clear that Alex's condition was not improving. In the end, he passed away peacefully, with Samantha by his side.

She was heartbroken, but also filled with gratitude for the time they had together. She knew that their love story was one for the ages, and that Alex would always be a part of her life, even though he was gone.

In the years that followed, Samantha continued to honour Alex's memory, living her life to the fullest and never taking a single moment for granted. She knew that Alex was watching over her, and that he was proud of everything she had accomplished.

And so, the story of Alex and Samantha lives on, a reminder that even in the face of tragedy, love can conquer all. Ears went by, but Samantha never forgot about Alex. His memory lived on in her heart, and she often found herself thinking about the life they could have had together.

But she refused to let her grief consume her. Instead, she channelled her pain into something positive, starting a foundation in Alex's memory to help others with rare illnesses.

The foundation quickly gained traction, and before she knew it, Samantha was traveling the world, speaking at conferences and spreading awareness about the importance of funding research for rare diseases.

Through it all, Alex was never far from her thoughts. She could still hear his voice in her head, cheering her on and urging her to keep fighting.

And then, one day, something miraculous happened. Samantha was in Paris, attending a conference on rare illnesses, when she met someone who took her breath away.

His name was Julien, and he was smart, funny, and charming. They talked for hours, and Samantha felt a spark she hadn't felt in years.

She knew that falling in love again would be difficult, but she also knew that Alex would want her to be happy. And so, she took a chance on Julien, and before she knew it, they were inseparable.

It wasn't always easy, of course. Samantha still struggled with feelings of guilt and sadness, knowing that Alex would never be far from her heart. But Julien was patient and understanding, and he never tried to replace Alex or make her forget about him.

Instead, he loved her for who she was, scars and all. And in time, Samantha realized that she could love him too, without betraying the memory of the man she had loved before.

Years went by, and Samantha and Julien continued to build a life together, filled with love, laughter, and adventure.

And though she knew that Alex would always hold a special place in her heart, she was grateful for the chance to love again.

Because in the end, that was what Alex had wanted for her all along - a love that endures, even in the face of adversity.

As Samantha looked out over the horizon, watching the sunset with Julien by her side, she knew that Alex was with her too, in spirit if not in body. And she smiled, remembering the words he had spoken to her so many years ago, when they were young and in love and full of hope.

*"I'll love you forever, Sam," he had said, his eyes shining with tears. "Even when I'm gone, my love will endure."*

And as the sun dipped below the horizon, Samantha felt the warmth of that love surround her, filling her heart with a sense of peace and contentment.

Because even though their story had ended in sadness, it had also been a story of great love, a love that had endured even in the face of death. And so, she whispered a thank you to Alex, for all the love and memories he had given her, and for the chance to find love again. Because in the end, that was what life was all about - loving and being loved, even in the face of tragedy and heartbreak.

And with that thought in her heart, Samantha turned to Julien and took his hand, ready to face whatever challenges lay ahead, secure in the knowledge that their love would endure, no matter what.

# The Magic and Romance

O ne of them was the king's advisor, a wise and cunning man named Marcus. He was initially against the idea of peace with William's kingdom, but Ellobarte's magic helped him see the error of his ways. He then became one of the biggest advocates for peace, working tirelessly to ensure that the two kingdoms could come together as one.

There was also a powerful sorceress named Selena, who lived in a tower on the edge of the kingdom. She was feared and respected by all, for her magical powers were unmatched. When she heard about Ellobarte's journey to bring peace, she was sceptical at first, but eventually came around and offered to use her powers to help.

As they worked towards peace, Isabella and William faced many challenges. There were those who still opposed the idea of peace, and they had to be dealt with. There were also natural disasters, such as floods and earthquakes, that threatened to derail their progress. But with the help of Ellobarte's, Marcus, Selena, and other allies, Isabella and William persevered.

They worked tirelessly to bring their people together, and in the end, they succeeded. The two kingdoms were united as one, and Isabella and William were able to marry and rule as one. As they grew older, Isabella and William faced new challenges.

They had children and grandchildren, and there were times when their family members disagreed about how to rule the kingdom. But they always remembered the lessons they learned about the importance of peace and unity, and they were able to guide their family and their people towards a better future.

And through it all, Ellobarte's watched over them, content in the knowledge that he had helped create a legacy of love and peace that would last for generations to come.

# Love in the Time

In the year 2060, the world had changed. War, famine, and disease had ravaged the planet, leaving only a handful of survivors. These survivors had banded together to form small communities, each with their own set of rules and beliefs.

In one of these communities, there lived a young woman named Sarah. She was strong and resourceful, with long red hair and piercing green eyes. She spent her days scavenging for food and supplies, and trying to keep herself and her small group of friends alive.

One day, as she was out on a mission, she met a man named Jake. He was tall and muscular, with short brown hair and a charming smile. They struck up a conversation, and over time, they fell deeply in love.

They spent their days exploring the ruins of the old world, talking about their hopes and dreams, and trying to build a better future for themselves and their community.

They were happy, but they both knew that something was missing. They longed to have a child, to bring new life into the world and give them a reason to keep fighting.

In this dystopian world, however, having a child was not a simple matter. Resources were scarce, and there were strict regulations in place to ensure that only those who could provide for a child were allowed to have one.

Sarah and Jake knew that they would have to go through a rigorous screening process, and even then, there was no guarantee that they would be approved. They decided to try anyway, and after months of waiting, they were finally given permission to have a child.

Nine months later, Sarah gave birth to a beautiful baby boy. They named him Adam, and they loved him with all their hearts. They raised him in a world where survival was the norm, and he grew up to be strong and resilient, just like his parents.

As Adam grew older, Sarah and Jake knew that it was time to let him go out into the world and find his own path. They knew that they had given him the best possible start in life, and they were proud of the person he had become.

But what lay ahead for Sarah and Jake, and for their community as a whole, was uncertain. They knew that resources were dwindling, and that their survival was not guaranteed. They knew that they would have to keep fighting, every day, just to stay alive.

And so, as Sarah and Jake watched their son leave the nest, they knew that their love had created something beautiful and lasting. They knew that their dystopian society had given them the opportunity to create a family and a legacy of love, and they felt grateful for the chance to be a part of it.

But what lay ahead for them was unknown. They knew that their love would always be strong, but they also knew that the future was uncertain. They would continue to fight, to survive, and to love, no matter what the world threw their way.

# Tongues of Love

In the heart of a bustling city, there lived a young woman named Maya. She was a writer, and spent her days weaving stories of passion and adventure. She was known for her vivid descriptions of love, and her ability to capture the essence of the human heart.

One day, as she was walking through the city, she met a man named Leo. He was an artist, with a wild mop of curly hair and a mischievous smile. Maya was immediately drawn to him, and they struck up a conversation about art and beauty.

As they talked, Maya realized that Leo was not like any man she had ever met before. The spoke of love in a way that was different from her own writing, and it intrigued her. He used words like "affection", "tenderness", and "devotion" to describe the feeling of being in love.

Maya was fascinated by Leo's use of these words, and she began to explore them in her own writing. She found that they brought a new depth and meaning to her stories, and she began to see love in a different light. As their relationship blossomed, Maya and Leo continued to explore different words for love.

They talked about "adoration", "cherishing", and "fondness". They discovered that each word carried its own unique meaning, and that they could use them to express their feelings in new and exciting ways.

Their love grew stronger with each passing day, and they knew that they were meant to be together. They continued to write and create, drawing inspiration from each other and from the world around them.

But as time went on, Maya began to realize that love was not just about words. It was about actions, and about showing your love in tangible ways. She started to understand the true meaning of "commitment", "loyalty", and "dedication".

As Maya and Leo faced challenges together, they relied on these words to guide them through the tough times.

They showed their love through their actions, and through the way they supported each other. And in the end, they knew that their love was something special.

It was a love that was expressed not just through words, but through actions and deeds. It was a love that had grown and evolved, and that would continue to do so for years to come.

# The Difficult to Departure

Carla and David had been together for two years. They met in college and fell in love over their shared love of music. David was a talented guitarist, while Carla had a beautiful singing voice. Together, they played in a band and performed at local gigs.

But as their relationship progressed, Carla began to feel restless. She loved David, but she also had dreams of traveling the world and experiencing new things. She felt like she was stuck in a rut, and that she needed to break free in order to truly find herself.

David, on the other hand, was content with their life together. He loved playing music with Carla and saw a future with her. He couldn't understand why she wanted to leave everything behind.

One day, Carla made the difficult decision to break up with David. She knew it would be hard, but she felt like it was the only way to live the life she wanted. David was devastated, but he respected Carla's decision. As time went on, Carla travelled the world and had many adventures.

She met new people and experienced different cultures. But no matter where she went or what she did, she couldn't shake the feeling that something was missing.

Meanwhile, David continued to play music and build a successful career. But he couldn't forget about Carla, and he wondered if he had made a mistake in letting her go. Years passed, and Carla and David lost touch. But one day, they ran into each other on the street. They hugged and caught up on each other's lives.

Carla was surprised to see how successful David had become, and she was impressed by his dedication to his music. David, on the other hand, was happy to see Carla again, but he could tell that something was different about her.

As they talked, Carla revealed that even though she had travelled the world and had many adventures, she still felt like something was missing. She realized that the thing she was looking for was right in front of her all along - her love for David.

David was overjoyed to hear this, but he was also hesitant. He didn't want to get hurt again, and he was worried about what would happen if they got back together. But Carla was determined to make it work. She knew that she had made a mistake in leaving David, and she was willing to do whatever it took to make things right. And so, they decided to give their relationship another chance.

It wasn't easy, but Carla and David worked hard to rebuild their relationship. They talked about their hopes and dreams, and they learned to compromise and support each other. And in the end, they knew that they were meant to be together.

# A Match Made the Fate

The sun began to set over the stadium, the roar of the crowd grew louder and louder. The two teams took the field, ready to battle it out in one of the most highly anticipated football matches of the year.

In the stands, two strangers sat next to each other, their eyes glued to the players on the field. Sarah was a die-hard fan of the home team, while Alex had come to support the opposing team.

Despite their different allegiances, Sarah and Alex couldn't help but strike up a conversation during the game. They talked about everything from the players on the field to their favourite foods and hobbies. As the game went on, they found themselves laughing and cheering together, caught up in the excitement of the moment.

As the clock wound down and the home team pulled ahead, Sarah and Alex shared a kiss, caught up in the rush of emotion. For the rest of the game, they held hands and whispered sweet nothings to each other, lost in their newfound love. But as the final whistle blew and the crowd began to disperse, Sarah and Alex both knew that their time together was limited.

They lived in different cities and had very different lives. They made promises to keep in touch, but they both knew that the reality of their situation was much more complicated.

Over the following days and weeks, Sarah and Alex exchanged text messages and phone calls, trying to maintain the connection they had built during the football match. But as time went on, their conversations grew shorter and less frequent. The reality of their distance and differences began to sink in, and they both knew that they would never be able to make things work.

In the end, Sarah and Alex decided to end things before they got too complicated. They said their goodbyes over the phone, promising to always remember the magical night they shared at the football match.

As Sarah hung up the phone, she couldn't help but feel a sense of sadness wash over her. She had truly fallen in love with Alex during that fateful night, but the timing and circumstances were simply not in their favour.

In the years that followed, Sarah would always remember the way she felt during that football match. She would think of Alex often, wondering what might have been if only things had been different. But deep down, she knew that the memory of that night would always be a cherished and bittersweet reminder of a love that could never be.

Months had passed since the football match, but Sarah still thought of Alex often. She had tried to move on, going out with friends and even going on a few dates, but no one could quite measure up to the connection she had felt with Alex.

One day, Sarah received an unexpected call from Alex. He was in town for a work conference and wanted to see if she was available to meet up.

Sarah was hesitant at first, but the thought of seeing Alex again was too tempting to resist. They made plans to meet up later that night at a local bar.

As she waited for Alex to arrive, Sarah's mind raced with all of the different scenarios that could play out. Would they rekindle their romance, or would they realize that they had moved on from each other? When Alex finally arrived, Sarah was struck by how handsome he still was. They hugged each other tightly, both of them feeling the familiar spark of attraction.

As they talked and caught up on each other's lives, Sarah couldn't help but feel like no time had passed at all.

They still had the same chemistry and connection that they had felt during the football match. But as the night wore on, Sarah began to sense that something was different about Alex.

He seemed distant and distracted, as if he had something weighing heavily on his mind.

When Sarah finally asked him what was wrong, Alex broke down in tears. He revealed that he had been diagnosed with a terminal illness and had only a few months left to live. Sarah was shocked and devastated by the news. She held Alex close, feeling the weight of his pain and sadness.

Over the next few months, Sarah and Alex spent as much time together as possible. They went on dates, travelled to new places, and made memories that would last a lifetime.

But as Alex's health began to decline, they both knew that their time together was limited. Sarah watched helplessly as Alex grew weaker and weaker, her heart breaking with every passing day.

Finally, on a beautiful autumn afternoon, Alex passed away peacefully in Sarah's arms. She was left with a heart full of love and memories, but also with a profound sense of loss.

As Sarah looked back on their time together, she realized that the football match had been just the beginning of their love story.

It had been a chance encounter that had led to a lifetime of love and heartbreak, a testament to the power of fate and destiny. And even though Alex was no longer with her, Sarah knew that their love would live on, a reminder of the magic and beauty that can be found in even the most unexpected of places.

# Science Fiction

# The Power of Uniqueness

## Chapter 1

Luna discovers a hidden cave where she finds a strange, glowing crystal. As she touches it, she is suddenly transported to a different planet, where she meets beings from all over the galaxy who share her lack of elemental control.

They reveal to her that she is part of a rare group of people who possess a unique power - the ability to bend reality itself.

With the help of her new friends, Luna learns to control her power and becomes a key player in a cosmic battle between good and evil.

Along the way, she discovers the true nature of her power and what it means to be different in a world where conformity is valued above all else.

As Luna journeys through the galaxy, she encounters strange and wonderful creatures, discovers hidden worlds, and faces unimaginable dangers. But through it all, she remains true to herself and her beliefs, inspiring others to embrace their own uniqueness and break free from the chains of societal expectations.

In the end, Luna returns to her home planet, armed with a new understanding of her place in the universe and the power of individuality.

She shows her people that there is more to life than elemental control, and that the power to shape one's own destiny lies within each of us.

Luna's story is one of courage, adventure, and the triumph of the human spirit in the face of adversity.

## Chapter 2

Luna returns to her home planet; she is met with hostility and scepticism from her community.

They view her newfound power as a threat to their way of life, and fear that it will upset the delicate balance of elemental control that they have maintained for centuries.

Despite their resistance, Luna refuses to back down. She uses her powers to help those in need, and to defend her people against the forces of darkness that threaten to destroy them.

With each victory, she gains more allies and inspires more individuals to embrace their own unique abilities.

Over time, Luna's actions begin to have an impact. Slowly but surely, her people begin to see the value in diversity and the power of individuality.

They start to question the rigid beliefs that have kept them divided for so long, and to open their minds to new possibilities.

As Luna's influence grows, she becomes a symbol of hope and inspiration to all those who have ever felt like they don't belong.

She shows them that there is strength in diversity, and that each person has the potential to make a difference in their own way.

In the end, Luna's journey leads her to a place of understanding and acceptance.

She realizes that her uniqueness is not a curse, but a gift - one that she can use to help others and to make the world a better place.

And with that knowledge, Luna continues to explore the vast expanse of the universe, ever curious and ever hopeful for what lies ahead.

## **Chapter 3**

Luna continues to explore the universe; she reflects on the lessons she has learned and the journey she has taken. And in a moment of clarity, she realizes the true meaning of her journey:

*"Being unique is not about fitting in, but standing out. It's about embracing your individuality and using it to make a difference in the world. We all have something special to offer, and it's up to us to find it and share it with others. So let us celebrate our differences, and use them to build a brighter, more inclusive future for all."*

# Lonely Lyra Tragic Odyssey

In a distant future, humanity has exhausted all of Earth's resources and is forced to look to the stars for survival. A group of astronauts is sent on a mission to find a new habitable planet, but the journey is long and dangerous. Among them is a young woman named Lyra, who has always dreamed of exploring the cosmos.

As the crew travels deeper into space, they encounter numerous challenges and setbacks. One by one, they begin to succumb to the harsh conditions of space travel, leaving Lyra alone and adrift in the vastness of the universe.

Despite her solitude, Lyra remains determined to complete her mission and find a new home for humanity. But as she gets closer to her goal, she realizes that the planet she has discovered is not what it seems. It is barren and lifeless, with no hope of sustaining human life.

Devastated by the realization that her mission has failed, Lyra is consumed by grief and despair.

She has sacrificed everything for a cause that was ultimately futile, and she is left with nothing but the emptiness of space. As she drifts aimlessly through the void, Lyra reflects on the fragility of human existence and the futility of our quest for survival

In the end, she realizes that the universe is vast and indifferent, and that our struggles and triumphs are ultimately insignificant in the grand scheme of things. And so, with a heavy heart and a profound sense of loss, Lyra floats off into the abyss, her fate unknown and her dreams unfulfilled. Her story is a tragic reminder of the fleeting nature of life and the inevitability of our own mortality.

"In the vast expanse of the cosmos, we are but fleeting sparks in an endless void. Our struggles and triumphs are but a brief flicker in the grand scheme of things, and our ultimate fate is to drift off into the abyss of time and space.

But even in our fleeting existence, we can find meaning and purpose, and strive to leave a lasting legacy that will endure long after we are gone.

# Star-Crossed Beyond the Cosmos

## Chapter 1

Pugal was a brilliant astrophysicist who spent his days studying the mysteries of the universe. He was a reserved and introspective person, more at home among the stars than among people. But that all changed when he met Yazhini.

Yazhini was a fiery and passionate astronomer who shared Pugal's love of the cosmos. She was everything he was not - outgoing, confident, and unafraid to speak her mind. From the moment they met, Pugal was captivated by her energy and enthusiasm.

As they worked together on various research projects, Pugal and Yazhini grew closer and their relationship deepened. They spent countless nights stargazing, sharing their dreams and hopes for the future.

But their romance was not without its challenges. Pugal's intense focus on his work often left Yazhini feeling neglected and alone.

And as they delved deeper into their research, they began to uncover troubling secrets about the universe that threatened to tear them apart.

As their relationship reached a crossroads, Pugal and Yazhini were faced with a choice - to continue down their separate paths or to forge a new future together. In a moment of clarity, they realized that their love for each other was stronger than any obstacle.

Together, they continued their work and uncovered ground-breaking discoveries that revolutionized the field of astrophysics.

And as they stood together, looking up at the stars, they knew that their love and their legacy would endure long after they were gone.

Pugal and Yazhini's story is a testament to the power of love and the wonders of the cosmos. They remind us that even in the vast expanse of the universe, there is always room for love and human connection.

## Chapter 2

Their careers soared, Pugal and Yazhini continued to explore the cosmos, driven by their insatiable curiosity and their love for each other.

They charted new galaxies and pushed the boundaries of what was thought possible, always together, always pushing each other to new heights.

But even as they achieved great success, they never lost sight of what was truly important - their relationship and their love for each other. They took the time to savour the small moments, to enjoy the beauty of the universe around them, and to nurture their connection.

As they grew older, their love only grew stronger, deepened by the experiences they shared and the challenges they faced. They became a beacon of hope and inspiration to others, proving that even in the face of great adversity, love and perseverance could conquer all.

And so, as they looked up at the stars one last time, their hands clasped tightly together, Pugal and Yazhini knew that they had lived a life full of wonder and meaning. Their legacy would endure, not just in the scientific discoveries they had made, but in the love, they had shared and the lives they had touched.

As Pugal whispered one final goodbye to Yazhini, he knew that their love would continue to guide him, even in the vast emptiness of space. And with that, he set off on one final journey, knowing that she would always be with him, in the stars and in his heart.

Their story reminds us that love is the most powerful force in the universe, capable of transcending time and space. And that in the end, it is the connections we make and the love we share that truly define us.

## **<u>Chapter 3</u>**

In the years that followed, Pugal continued to honour Yazhini's memory by pursuing their shared passion for astrophysics. He published groundbreaking research papers and made numerous significant discoveries that expanded humanity's understanding of the universe.

But despite his many achievements, Pugal never forgot the love that he and Yazhini had shared. He continued to feel her presence in the stars, in the very fabric of the universe they had both devoted their lives to studying.

As he looked up at the night sky, he could almost hear her voice, whispering to him of the wonders of the cosmos. And though he knew that he would never see her again in this life, he was comforted by the knowledge that they would one day be reunited among the stars. And so, as Pugal continued his work, he remained forever grateful for the love he had shared with Yazhini.

He knew that it had changed him in ways he could never fully comprehend, and that it had shaped the course of his life in ways he could never have imagined.

As he gazed up at the stars, he knew that he was not alone. For Yazhini was with him always, in every star, every planet, every nebula that he studied. And in that knowledge, he found solace, comfort, and the inspiration to continue his journey, always looking up, always seeking to understand the mysteries of the universe, and always guided by the love he had shared with his beloved Yazhini.

## **Chapter 4**

As Pugal looked up at the stars, he felt a sense of peace wash over him. And in that moment, he knew that he had found his place in the universe. For he had been touched by the greatest force of all - the power of love. And as he gazed up at the stars, he whispered one final quote, knowing that it was the legacy he and Yazhini had left behind:

*"The stars may seem distant and unattainable, but in truth, they are the embodiment of the greatest force in the universe - the power of love."*

# Interstellar Betrayal

## Chapter 1

D r. Emily Chen was a brilliant scientist who had dedicated her life to studying the mysteries of the universe. She had always been fascinated by the idea that there could be other intelligent life out there, and had spent countless hours analysing signals from distant planets, looking for any sign of extra-terrestrial communication.

But when she received a strange transmission from a nearby star system, Emily knew that she had stumbled upon something truly extraordinary.

The signal was unlike anything she had ever seen before - a series of complex mathematical equations, woven together in a pattern that seemed to defy explanation.

Determined to unravel the mystery, Emily devoted all her time and resources to decoding the transmission. As she worked tirelessly in her lab, she began to notice strange things happening around her. Her equipment would sometimes malfunction without explanation, and she would occasionally catch glimpses of strange figures moving in the shadows.

At first, Emily dismissed these occurrences as mere coincidences, but as they continued to escalate, she began to realize that something was very wrong.

She knew that she was being watched, but she couldn't figure out who or why. As Emily delved deeper into the transmission, she began to uncover a dark and sinister truth.

## **Chapter 2**

The signal was not a message of peace or friendship, but a warning of impending doom. The aliens who had sent it were in grave danger, and they needed Emily's help to survive.

Desperate to save these mysterious beings, Emily reached out to a team of experts in various scientific fields, hoping to piece together the puzzle and find a way to help the aliens. But as they worked together, they realized that there was more at stake than they had ever imagined. For the beings behind the transmission were not the benevolent creatures they had initially seemed to be.

In fact, they were the architects of a sinister plot to take over the Earth, using their advanced technology to subjugate humanity and turn the planet into a mere pawn in their interstellar game of conquest.

As the pieces of the puzzle fell into place, Emily and her team found themselves in a race against time to stop the alien threat before it was too late.

But with the fate of the planet hanging in the balance, and with the shadowy figures closing in around her, Emily knew that she would have to make the ultimate sacrifice to save humanity from its extra-terrestrial foes.

In the end, as the aliens descended upon the Earth, Emily stood alone, facing the greatest challenge of her life. And as she looked up at the sky, she whispered a final quote, knowing that her sacrifice would be remembered forever:

"In the face of darkness, we must always strive to find the light. And though the road ahead may be long and treacherous, we must never lose sight of the hope that guides us."

# Chapter 3

Emily stood before the alien invasion force; she knew that the fate of humanity rested on her shoulders. She had uncovered the truth about the aliens' plans, and she had prepared a desperate plan to stop them.

Using her knowledge of the transmission, Emily had designed a weapon that could disrupt the aliens' technology, rendering their ships useless. But to use it, she would have to expose herself to a massive dose of radiation, one that would surely kill her.

Taking a deep breath, Emily activated the weapon, feeling the radiation course through her body. As the aliens' ships began to falter and crash, she knew that her sacrifice had been worth it.

But even as she fell to the ground, Emily could sense that something was wrong.

The shadows around her were growing darker, and she could hear strange whispers in her ear.

It was then that she realized the terrible truth. The aliens had not been the only ones watching her.

There was a force far older and more malevolent lurking in the shadows, waiting to claim her soul.

With her dying breath, Emily whispered a final quote, hoping that it would serve as a warning to others:

*"The universe is a place of wonders and terrors beyond our comprehension. And though we may strive to understand its mysteries, we must always be wary of the darkness that lies in wait."*

# Drama & Tragedy

# Farewell on the Tracks

Yumi and Tatsuya sat side-by-side on the train, staring out at the passing Japanese countryside. They had been traveling together for weeks, exploring the country and immersing themselves in the culture. As the train rattled along the tracks, Yumi couldn't help but feel a sense of unease.

Suddenly, the train lurched to a stop, jolting Yumi and Tatsuya out of their seats. They looked out the window and saw that the tracks ahead had been completely destroyed, as if by a great explosion. Panic set in as they realized they were stranded in the middle of nowhere with no way to call for help.

As the hours passed, Yumi and Tatsuya began to feel the weight of their situation. They had no food or water, and the sun was starting to set. Just as they were about to lose hope, they heard a voice calling out to them.

They followed the voice to a nearby village, where they were greeted by a group of kind-hearted people who took them in and provided them with food and shelter. But as they settled into their new surroundings, Yumi and Tatsuya began to notice that something was not quite right.

The villagers seemed to be living in fear of a powerful sorceress who lived deep in the forest. They told Yumi and Tatsuya stories of her dark magic and the terrible things she had done to those who crossed her path.

Despite the warnings, Yumi and Tatsuya were determined to help the villagers. They set out into the forest, hoping to find a way to defeat the sorceress and restore peace to the village.

As they journeyed deeper into the forest, they encountered many dangers and obstacles, but they never gave up. Finally, they reached the sorceress's lair and engaged her in a fierce battle.

Yumi and Tatsuya fought with all their might, but in the end, the sorceress proved to be too powerful. Tatsuya was struck down in the battle, leaving Yumi to fight on her own. With tears in her eyes, Yumi unleashed a powerful spell that defeated the sorceress, but it came at a great cost.

Tatsuya lay motionless on the ground, and no amount of magic or medicine could bring him back to life. As Yumi mourned the loss of her friend, she knew that she had fulfilled her mission. The village was free from the sorceress's tyranny, and the people were finally able to live in peace.

But as Yumi boarded the train to leave the village behind, she couldn't shake the feeling of sadness that clung to her heart. She knew that her journey with Tatsuya had come to an end, but she couldn't help but wonder what other adventures they might have had together if only he had survived.

And so, Yumi sat alone on the train, watching the countryside pass by as she mourned the loss of her friend and the bittersweet end to their journey together.

# The Uncharted Seas

The shipping industry was a world unto itself, a place where danger and excitement lurked around every corner. And for Olivia, a young engineer fresh out of college, it was a world that held endless possibilities.

Olivia had always been fascinated by ships and the sea. She had grown up in a coastal town, watching the giant cargo ships come and go from the harbour. It was a place where dreams were made and fortunes were won, and Olivia was determined to be a part of it. When she landed her first job on a cargo ship, Olivia couldn't believe her luck.

She was thrilled to be working alongside experienced engineers and deckhands, learning everything she could about the inner workings of the ship.

But as the weeks turned into months, Olivia began to realize that life at sea was not all smooth sailing. She worked long hours, sometimes up to 18 hours a day, and the work was often gruelling and dangerous. Despite the challenges, Olivia found herself drawn to the ruggedly handsome first mate, Jack.

They would steal moments together on the deck, stealing kisses in the moonlight and sharing whispered secrets. But as they grew closer, Olivia began to suspect that Jack was hiding something from her. He would often disappear for hours at a time, leaving her alone to manage the ship's machinery and systems.

One night, as they sat on the deck under the stars, Olivia finally confronted Jack about his mysterious absences. He revealed that he was working with a group of smugglers, sneaking illegal goods across international borders.

Olivia was shocked and dismayed by the revelation. She had always known that the shipping industry was a dangerous one, but she had never imagined that she would be caught up in something so illegal and dangerous. As she struggled to come to terms with the truth, Olivia found herself torn between her love for Jack and her sense of duty to do the right thing.

She knew that she had to report the smuggling operation to the authorities, but she couldn't bear the thought of betraying Jack.

In the end, Olivia made the difficult decision to turn Jack in. It was a painful and heart-wrenching choice, but she knew that it was the right thing to do. As Jack was arrested and taken away, Olivia was left alone to manage the ship and navigate the treacherous waters. It was a lonely and isolating experience, but she knew that she had to stay strong and focused.

Months later, as Olivia stepped off the ship and onto solid ground, she knew that her life would never be the same. She had been through an experience that had tested her limits and challenged her sense of right and wrong. But she had also found a sense of purpose and determination that she had never known before.

She looked out at the sea; Olivia knew that she had found her true calling. The shipping industry may have been dangerous and unpredictable, but it was also a place where dreams could come true and where anything was possible. And for Olivia, that was a world worth fighting for.

# The Mermaid Plea

In a small village nestled in the heart of a dense forest, there lived a young woman named Eira. She had always felt a deep connection to the natural world and the creatures that lived within it, and had spent her entire life exploring the woods and communing with the animals.

One day, while on a walk in the forest, Eira stumbled upon a hidden grove. It was unlike any place she had ever seen before; the trees were taller and more ancient, the air was thick with the scent of wildflowers, and a sense of magic seemed to permeate the air.

As Eira explored the grove, she felt drawn to a small pond at its centre. She gazed into the still waters, and saw a vision of a beautiful mermaid, her hair flowing like seaweed and her eyes sparkling like diamonds.

The mermaid spoke to Eira, telling her that she had been searching for someone who could help her. She explained that her underwater kingdom was in peril, threatened by an evil sorceress who had seized control of the ocean's magical powers.

Eira was hesitant at first, but the mermaid's plea touched her heart. She knew that she had to help, no matter the cost. Together, Eira and the mermaid set out on a perilous journey to the underwater kingdom. Along the way, they encountered all manner of dangerous creatures, from giant sea monsters to treacherous pirates.

As they approached the kingdom, Eira could feel the sorceress's dark magic pulsing through the water. She steeled herself for the battle ahead, determined to save the mermaid's home and all the creatures that called it home.

The battle was fierce and intense, with spells and curses flying through the water like lightning bolts. But Eira was not afraid; she had the magic of the forest flowing through her veins, and the strength of the mermaid's love behind her.

In the end, Eira emerged victorious, and the sorceress was defeated. The underwater kingdom was safe once again, and the mermaid and her people rejoiced. As Eira prepared to return to her own world, the mermaid appeared before her once again.

She thanked Eira for her bravery and sacrifice, and offered her a gift - the ability to communicate with animals in a way that no other human ever could.

Eira returned to her village a changed woman, with a newfound sense of purpose and power. She spent the rest of her days wandering the woods, helping the creatures she loved and protecting the natural world from harm.

And though she never forgot her time in the underwater kingdom, she knew that her true home was in the forest, among the trees and the animals she loved so deeply.

# The Power of Choice

Sophie had always been a bit of a rebel. She lived life on her own terms, refusing to conform to anyone else's expectations. It was this attitude that had led her to leave her small hometown and move to the city, where she could be free to pursue her dreams.

It was in the city that she met Jake. He was everything Sophie wasn't - quiet, reserved, and always playing it safe. But something about him drew her in, and before she knew it, they were inseparable.

For years, they lived a happy life together, building a home and a family. But as time went on, Sophie began to feel restless. She longed for adventure, for something more than the mundane routine of their daily lives.

One day, while out on a walk, she met a mysterious stranger. He was tall and handsome, with piercing green eyes and a voice that sent shivers down her spine. The spoke of a life of excitement and danger, of travel and exploration. Sophie felt herself drawn to him, unable to resist the pull of his magnetic presence.

They began a passionate affair, meeting in secret and indulging in all manner of wild and reckless behaviour.

As the weeks turned into months, Sophie found herself torn between the life she had built with Jake and the exhilaration of her new lover. She knew that she had to make a choice, but the decision weighed heavily on her heart.

The day of reckoning finally arrived when Jake discovered her infidelity. He was devastated, and Sophie was wracked with guilt. She tried to explain herself, to tell him that she still loved him and that she was just going through a phase, but it was too late.

Jake made the difficult decision to end their relationship, and Sophie was left alone with nothing but her regret and her memories.

In the end, it was up to the reader to decide Sophie's fate. Would she stay in the city and continue her reckless ways, or would she find her way back to Jake and try to make things, right? The ending was left open to interpretation, a reflection of the reader's own hopes and fears for the future.

Despite the painful ending of her relationship with Jake, Sophie continued to live life on her own terms. She threw herself into her work, pursuing her dreams with a renewed vigoro.

It wasn't long before she caught the eye of a powerful business mogul, who offered her a job in his company. Sophie was hesitant at first, but the salary and benefits were too good to pass up. She accepted the offer and found herself quickly rising through the ranks.

As she climbed the corporate ladder, Sophie found herself drawn into a world of power and intrigue. She made new friends and enemies, navigating the tricky waters of office politics with ease. But deep down, she couldn't shake the feeling that something was missing. She longed for the days of her youth, when she had been carefree and unburdened by the weight of responsibility.

One day, while on a business trip to a far-off city, Sophie met a wise old woman. The woman saw through Sophie's facade, sensing the sadness and longing that she tried so hard to hide.

"You are a woman torn between two worlds," the old woman said. "You have tasted the forbidden fruit of excitement and danger, and now you must decide where your true path lies."

Sophie was taken aback by the woman's insight. She knew that she had been living a double life, trying to balance the demands of her job with the yearning in her heart.

She boarded the plane back home; Sophie made a decision. She would leave her job, leave the city, and start anew. She would travel the world, seeking out adventure and following her heart wherever it led.

The ending of Sophie's story was left once again to the reader's interpretation. Would she find the fulfilment she sought, or would she regret her decision to leave her old life behind? It was up to each individual to decide for themselves.

# The Love and Betrayal

Natalie was a bright and ambitious young woman with a promising future ahead of her. She had just graduated from college with honours and landed a prestigious job at a top firm in the city.

Despite her many accomplishments, Natalie was haunted by a dark secret from her past. When she was a child, she had witnessed the murder of her parents in a brutal home invasion. The experience had left her traumatized and emotionally scarred.

Natalie had never fully recovered from the tragedy, but she had learned to bury her pain deep inside and carry on with her life. She threw herself into her work, hoping to find solace and purpose in her career.

For a while, everything seemed to be going well. Natalie's career was thriving, and she was making a name for herself in her field.

She even met a kind and loving man named Michael, who seemed to understand her in a way that no one else ever had. But one day, Natalie's world came crashing down around her.

A shocking revelation from her past threatened to destroy everything she had worked so hard to build. It turned out that the man she had been dating, Michael, was actually the son of the man who had killed her parents. Michael had known the truth all along but had kept it hidden from Natalie, fearing that she would reject him if she knew.

Natalie was devastated by the news. She felt like her life had been nothing but a lie, and that she had been betrayed by the one person she had trusted more than anyone else.

In her despair, Natalie made a fateful decision. She would take her own life, ending the pain and suffering that had plagued her for so long.

The news of Natalie's death sent shockwaves through her community. Her colleagues and friends were left reeling, struggling to understand how someone so talented and promising could have come to such a tragic end.

Natalie's story was a reminder of the power of the past to shape our present and our future. It was a cautionary tale of how even the brightest stars can be extinguished by the weight of our own demons.

As news of Natalie's death spread, Michael was consumed by guilt and remorse. He realized too late the devastating impact his deception had on her and how it had contributed to her tragic end.

Michael could not bear to live with the weight of his actions, and he, too, decided to end his life. His death only added to the sense of loss and tragedy surrounding Natalie's passing. In the wake of the tragedy, many questions remained unanswered.

People wondered how someone as talented and accomplished as Natalie could have been driven to take her own life. Others questioned how Michael could have kept such a terrible secret from the woman he claimed to love. But despite the confusion and sorrow, there was also a glimmer of hope.

Natalie's death served as a wake-up call to those around her, a reminder that life is fragile and fleeting, and that we must cherish every moment while we can.

In the years that followed, Natalie's memory lived on, not just as a cautionary tale but as a reminder of the power of love, forgiveness, and second chances.

Her tragic story had touched the hearts of many and had inspired countless others to live their lives to the fullest, no matter what obstacles they faced.

# Whispers from Beyond

Ava had always been fascinated by the supernatural. She spent her days poring over books on ghosts, witches, and other creatures of the night, hoping to uncover some hidden truth about the world around her.

One night, as she was walking home from the library, Ava stumbled upon an ancient graveyard hidden deep in the woods. As she wandered through the graves, she felt a strange energy coursing through her, as if the spirits of the dead were calling out to her.

Suddenly, she saw him: a handsome young man standing at the edge of the clearing. His eyes were dark and intense, and she felt drawn to him in a way she couldn't explain.

The man's name was Ethan, and he was a ghost who had been haunting the graveyard for centuries. Ava was intrigued by him, and they began to meet each night, talking for hours about everything and nothing. As time went on, Ava found herself falling deeply in love with Ethan, despite the fact that he was a ghost and they could never truly be together. She longed to touch him, to feel his lips against hers, but she knew it was impossible.

One day, Ava discovered that there was a way for her and Ethan to be together. A powerful witch who lived in the nearby woods had the ability to bring the dead back to life, and Ava knew that this was her only chance to be with the man she loved.

She sought out the witch and begged her to bring Ethan back to life. The witch agreed, but warned Ava that there would be consequences for her actions.

Despite the warnings, Ava went ahead with the plan, and Ethan was brought back to life. They were finally able to be together, but Ava soon realized that the consequences were more than she could bear.

The witch had cursed her, and she began to experience terrifying visions of the dead, haunting her day and night. Ethan tried to help her, but the curse was too strong, and Ava realized that the only way to break it was to give up her own life.

In a final act of sacrifice, Ava willingly gave up her life, breaking the curse and freeing herself from the haunting visions. Ethan was heartbroken, but he knew that Ava had done what was necessary to save herself.

In the end, Ethan returned to the graveyard, haunted once again by his eternal existence, but grateful for the time he had been able to spend with the woman he loved.

# A Small Smile that Changes Everything

A young girl who dreams of becoming a professional ballerina. She works tirelessly for years, training rigorously and sacrificing social events and leisure time. Finally, she lands the lead role in a prestigious ballet company's production, and her excitement is palpable. But on the day of the performance, she slips and falls, shattering her ankle and ending her dance career.

However, a single line can take a tragic story to an even deeper level of sorrow and heartbreak. As the young girl lies on the hospital bed, staring at the ceiling in disbelief, her doctor enters the room and delivers the crushing news,

"I'm sorry, but you'll never dance again."

The girl's world crumbles around her as she realizes that her lifelong dream has been ripped away from her in an instant. She feels lost and hopeless, wondering what her life will be like without the thing she loves most. And yet, despite her devastation, she tries to muster a small smile as she remembers the countless hours of joy and fulfilment that dancing had given her.

As the days pass, the young girl's smile becomes harder and harder to summon. She is consumed by grief and despair, unable to find solace in anything. Her once-bright future now seems bleak and hopeless. But then, a small act of kindness from a stranger begins to change everything.

One day, as the girl is sitting alone in the hospital cafeteria, feeling more alone than ever before, a woman approaches her with a warm smile and a kind heart. She strikes up a conversation with the girl, listening intently as she shares her story of loss and heartbreak. The woman offers words of comfort and encouragement, telling the girl that she is strong and capable of overcoming any obstacle.

For the first time in weeks, the girl feels a glimmer of hope. She begins to open up to the woman, sharing her fears and doubts.

The woman listens patiently, offering guidance and support. Slowly but surely, the girl begins to regain her sense of purpose.

She realizes that while she may never dance again, she can still find happiness and fulfilment in other areas of her life. She starts to explore new hobbies and interests, discovering a passion for writing and art.

Years later, the young girl looks back on that fateful day with mixed emotions. It was a day that had brought her to the lowest point in her life, but it was also the day that had set her on a new path.

She remembers the small smile that had once been so easy to summon, and how it had been replaced by tears and heartache. But now, as she thinks of the woman who had shown her kindness and compassion, the girl feels a new sense of gratitude and hope. She realizes that while life can be cruel and unpredictable, there is always the potential for goodness and light.

As time passes, the young girl's passion for writing and art blossoms, and she begins to share her talents with the world.

She writes and illustrates children's books, sharing messages of hope and resilience with young readers. Her work becomes widely popular, and she receives countless letters from children and adults alike, telling her how much her books have touched their lives.

One day, while attending a book signing event, the young girl meets a man who introduces himself as a dance instructor. They strike up a conversation, and the young girl shares her story of how she once dreamed of becoming a professional ballerina. The man listens intently, and then offers to give her a private dance lesson. The young girl is hesitant at first, but then she remembers the woman who had shown her kindness in the hospital all those years ago. She realizes that life is full of unexpected opportunities, and that she should never give up on her dreams.

The young girl accepts the dance lesson, and as she begins to move her body once again, she feels a sense of joy and freedom that she hasn't felt in years. She realizes that while her ankle may never fully heal, she can still find ways to express herself through movement.

She continues to take dance lessons with the instructor, and eventually starts teaching her own dance classes for children. Years later, the young girl looks back on her journey with pride and gratitude.

She realizes that her life took a different path than she had once imagined, but that it is a path full of love, joy, and fulfilment. She remembers the small smile that had once brightened up her day, and she knows that it was just the beginning of a journey that would lead her to a happy and meaningful life.

# Horror & Fantasy

# The Haunting and Tale of Love

## Chapter 1

Yazhini walked into the old, dilapidated house; she could feel the chill of the air creeping up her spine. She had come to visit the house with her husband, Pugal, who had grown up in the neighbourhood. Pugal had always been fascinated by the old mansion, which had been abandoned for decades, and he was eager to explore its hidden secrets.

As they walked through the creaky halls and dusty rooms, Yazhini couldn't shake the feeling that they were not alone. She heard whispers in the shadows and footsteps on the stairs, but when she turned to look, there was nobody there.

And they made their way to the top floor, Pugal suddenly froze in his tracks.

He turned to Yazhini and said, "Do you feel that?" Yazhini felt the hair on her arms stand up as a cold breeze blew through the hallway. They heard a faint whisper, and Yazhini could see a figure in the distance. As they moved closer, they realized it was Pugal's ghostly doppelganger.

The ghost of Pugal looked just like him, but his face was twisted into a sinister grin. Yazhini tried to run, but she found herself rooted to the spot. The ghost of Pugal approached her slowly, his eyes glowing with a malevolent light. She could hear his voice in her head, taunting her, promising to never let her go.

As the ghost of Pugal drew closer, Yazhini suddenly heard a voice from behind her. It was the voice of Pugal, her real husband. He had come back to the house to find her, and he had brought a team of paranormal investigators with him.

The investigators quickly took control of the situation and managed to banish the ghost of Pugal from the house. As they left the mansion, Yazhini and Pugal looked back at the old, haunted house, grateful to be alive and together.

But as they walked away, Yazhini couldn't help but wonder what other secrets lay hidden within the walls of the old mansion. And she knew that they would never be truly safe until the ghost of Pugal was finally put to rest.

# Chapter 2

Over the next few days, Yazhini couldn't shake the feeling of dread that had settled over her. She couldn't sleep at night and was haunted by nightmares of the ghost of Pugal. She felt like she was losing her grip on reality.

Pugal tried to comfort her, but he didn't understand the depth of her fear. He thought that the incident at the old house was just a freak occurrence and that they were safe now.

But Yazhini knew better. She could feel the ghost of Pugal lurking just beyond the edges of her vision, waiting to strike.

One night, as she was lying in bed, Yazhini felt a cold hand reach out and touch her shoulder. She tried to scream, but no sound came out.

She felt a presence in the room, an evil energy that seemed to be feeding off her fear. Suddenly, the door burst open, and Pugal rushed in, followed by the paranormal investigators.

They had come to help her. Using their expertise, the investigators were able to banish the ghost of Pugal for good. Yazhini could feel the oppressive energy in the room dissipate, and she finally felt safe again. But the experience had changed her forever.

She knew that ghosts and spirits were real, and that they could be dangerous. She also realized how much she loved Pugal and how much she was willing to fight for their love.

In the end, Yazhini and Pugal emerged from the experience stronger and more united than ever before. They knew that they had been through something terrifying together, and they were grateful to be alive and, in each other's arms.

## **Chapter 3**

As the days passed, Yazhini and Pugal tried to put the experience behind them and move on with their lives. But the memory of the ghostly encounter lingered in their minds, and they couldn't shake the feeling that they were being watched.

One evening, as they were sitting in their living room watching TV, Yazhini felt a cold breeze blow through the room. She turned to Pugal and saw that he had gone pale.

They both knew what that meant: the ghost of Pugal had returned. They quickly contacted the paranormal investigators, who rushed over to their home to help them. The investigators brought with them an array of tools and equipment to help them track down the ghost and banish it once and for all.

As they began their investigation, Yazhini and Pugal watched nervously from the side-lines. They could hear strange noises coming from the other room, and they felt a chill in the air.

Suddenly, one of the investigators let out a loud scream. Yazhini and Pugal rushed over to see what had happened and found the investigator lying on the floor, seemingly unconscious.

They quickly realized that the ghost of Pugal was more powerful than they had anticipated. The investigators regrouped and came up with a new plan, one that would hopefully be strong enough to banish the ghost for good.

## **Chapter 4**

They began a ritual that involved chanting and burning special herbs. As they chanted, the room began to fill with a thick, white mist, and Yazhini could feel the energy in the air shifting.

Finally, with a burst of light and a loud bang, the ghost of Pugal disappeared. Yazhini and Pugal collapsed onto the couch, exhausted but relieved that the ordeal was finally over. As they sat there catching their breath, they looked at each other with a newfound appreciation for the fragility of life. They knew that they had been given a second chance, and they were determined to make the most of it.

From that day forward, Yazhini and Pugal lived their lives to the fullest, cherishing every moment together and never taking anything for granted.

They knew that they had faced their greatest fears and emerged victorious, and they were grateful for every day that they had together.

## **Chapter 5**

Despite banishing the ghost of Pugal, Yazhini and Pugal couldn't escape the feeling of unease that had settled over them. They knew that the spirit world was unpredictable, and they feared that the ghost might return once again.

They decided to take action and sought out the help of a spiritual healer. The healer was a wise woman who had spent her entire life studying the mysteries of the spirit world. After conducting a thorough investigation, the healer confirmed their worst fears: the ghost of Pugal was still haunting them. But she also had a plan to banish the ghost for good. She instructed

Yazhini and Pugal to gather a number of special ingredients, including rare herbs and crystals, and to perform a ritual at the site of the original haunting.

Together, Yazhini and Pugal followed the healer's instructions to the letter.

They created a sacred circle, burned special herbs, and chanted ancient incantations. As they chanted, they could feel the energy in the air shifting once again.

They felt a powerful presence in the room, and Yazhini could sense the ghost of Pugal trying to resist. But with a final burst of energy, the ritual was complete. The ghost of Pugal was banished for good, and Yazhini and Pugal could finally breathe a sigh of relief.

They thanked the spiritual healer for her help and vowed to never forget the lessons that they had learned.

They knew that the spirit world was a powerful and unpredictable force, but they also knew that they had the strength and the determination to face any challenge that came their way.

# Chapter 6

From that day forward, Yazhini and Pugal lived their lives with a newfound appreciation for the mysteries of the universe. They knew that they had been given a second chance, and they were determined to make the most of it.

They cherished every moment together, never taking anything for granted, and always staying mindful of the power of the spirit world. And so, the story of Yazhini and Pugal's encounter with the ghost came to an end. Though they had faced their greatest fears and emerged victorious, they knew that they would never forget the experience.

From that day forward, they lived their lives with a deeper understanding of the mysteries of the universe. They knew that there were forces beyond their control, but they also knew that they had the power to face them head-on.

They continued to cherish every moment together, never taking anything for granted, and always staying mindful of the power of the spirit world.

And they lived happily ever after, always remembering the lessons that they had learned and the challenges that they had overcome

# House in the Mountains

In a small town nestled in the mountains, there was an abandoned house that no one dared to enter. The locals whispered that the house was cursed, and that anyone who dared to step foot inside would never come out again.

One day, a group of teenagers decided to explore the house for a thrill. They broke in through a window and began to explore the dusty, cobweb-filled rooms. As they climbed the stairs to the second floor, they heard a faint whispering sound coming from one of the rooms.

Curiosity getting the better of them, they cautiously opened the door and saw a strange, glowing orb hovering in the centre of the room. The orb grew brighter and brighter until it filled the entire room with a blinding light.

When the light faded, the teenagers found themselves in a different room altogether, one that looked like it had been frozen in time. The walls were covered in faded wallpaper, and there was an old-fashioned rotary phone on a nearby table.

As they were exploring the room, the phone suddenly rang. One of the teenagers hesitantly answered it, only to hear a voice on the other end that sounded like it was coming from another world.

The voice spoke in a language that the teenagers couldn't understand, but its tone was menacing and filled with malice. Suddenly, the room began to shake violently, and the teenagers realized that they were trapped in a terrifying alternate dimension.

They tried to leave the room, but the door wouldn't budge. As they huddled together, praying for a way out, they saw shadowy figures materialize around them, slowly closing in.

The last thing the teenagers heard was the sound of the phone ringing in the empty room, as they were consumed by the darkness. To this day, no one knows what became of the teenagers who dared to enter the cursed house.

# Phantoms on the Top Floor

In the heart of a bustling city, there was a tall, imposing building that stood out among the rest. No one knew who owned it or what it was used for, but rumours circulated that it was haunted by the ghosts of its former inhabitants.

One night, a group of friends decided to explore the building, despite the warnings of locals. They broke in through a side entrance and began to climb the stairs to the top floor. As they ascended, they felt an eerie presence watching them, and heard strange noises coming from the floors below.

When they reached the top floor, they found a single room, illuminated only by the light of the moon shining through a cracked window. In the centre of the room was a strange object, pulsating with an otherworldly energy.

The friends cautiously approached the object, but as they got closer, they felt an overwhelming sense of dread.

Suddenly, the object began to glow brighter and brighter, until it was too bright to look at. When the light faded, the friends found themselves in a different room altogether. This room was dimly lit, and filled with old, dusty furniture.

But as they looked closer, they saw that the furniture was covered in cobwebs, and that the room had been abandoned for years.

As they explored the room, they began to feel a sense of unease. It was as if the room was alive, and was watching them with malevolent intent. Suddenly, they heard a faint whispering sound, coming from a dark corner of the room.

As they approached the corner, they saw a shadowy figure materialize before them. It was the ghost of a woman, dressed in a long, flowing gown.

She beckoned to them with a bony finger, and as they drew closer, they saw that her eyes were black pits, devoid of any life.

The friends tried to flee, but the door wouldn't budge. They were trapped, with no escape from the ghostly apparition. They screamed and cried for help, but no one came to their aid.

In the end, they were consumed by the darkness, and became trapped in the haunted building forevermore. And to this day, the building still stands, a monument to the horror that lies within.

# The Dollmaker Revenge

A family moved into a new house in the countryside, hoping to start a new life away from the city. They were overjoyed to find a beautiful old farmhouse with plenty of land, surrounded by lush forests. But soon after moving in, strange things began to happen. The family heard strange noises in the night, footsteps in the hallways, and doors opening and closing on their own.

They tried to ignore it at first, telling themselves that it was just the creaks and groans of an old house. But things took a turn for the worse when their youngest daughter began talking to an imaginary friend. The family assumed it was just a phase, until they began to hear her talking to the imaginary friend at night, in her sleep.

They heard her giggling and whispering to the friend, even though no one was there.

One night, the family woke up to find their daughter missing from her bed. They searched the house and the surrounding woods for hours, but she was nowhere to be found. As they were about to give up hope, they heard her voice calling out from the woods.

They followed the voice to a clearing, where they saw their daughter standing next to a tall, shadowy figure. The figure had glowing eyes and sharp, pointed teeth, and it was beckoning to the girl.

The family tried to run, but they found themselves trapped in the clearing, unable to escape. The figure slowly approached them, its eyes fixed on the youngest daughter. As it drew closer, the family realized that they were face-to-face with a demonic entity, one that had been living in the house long before they arrived.

The entity possessed the daughter, using her body as a vessel to wreak havoc on the family. They were never seen or heard from again, and the house remained empty for years, a warning to anyone who dared to enter.

# Unleashed Nightmare

In a faraway land, a young sorceress named Lyra discovered an ancient grimoire that was said to hold the power to bring forth unspeakable horrors. Despite the warnings of her mentor, she delved deep into the book, eager to unlock its secrets.

As she read the dark incantations, she felt a surge of power coursing through her veins. She raised her hands, and in an instant, the ground beneath her shook and a dark portal opened before her.

From the portal emerged a horde of twisted creatures, born from the darkest depths of the abyss. Lyra tried to close the portal, but it was too late. The creatures had already spilled into the world, spreading chaos and destruction in their wake.

Lyra knew she had made a grave mistake, but it was too late to undo the damage she had caused. She set out on a quest to right her wrongs, searching for a way to banish the creatures back to the abyss from which they had come. As she journeyed through the land, she encountered a wise old druid who offered to help her in her quest.

Together, they travelled to the heart of the dark forest, where they discovered an ancient tree, rumoured to hold the power to undo the sorceress's terrible mistake.

Lyra and the druid performed a powerful ritual, calling upon the forces of nature to aid them in their battle against the dark forces that had invaded their world.

They battled the twisted creatures, one by one, until they stood before the portal that had brought them forth. With a final burst of magic, Lyra summoned the strength to close the portal, banishing the creatures back to the abyss from which they had come.

But as she turned to leave, she realized that the darkness had taken its toll on her, leaving her forever scarred by the horrors she had unleashed.

From that day forward, Lyra vowed to use her magic only for the forces of good, never again dabbling in the dark arts that had brought such terror to her world.

# The Silent Echoes

A group of friends decided to take a weekend camping trip deep in the wilderness, away from the hustle and bustle of city life. They set up camp near a quiet, tranquil lake and spent the day hiking and fishing.

As the night fell, the friends sat around a campfire, telling stories and roasting marshmallows. But as they were about to go to sleep, they noticed something strange happening in the lake.

The water began to glow, emitting a faint, ethereal light that seemed to dance on the surface of the lake. The friends were intrigued, and they decided to investigate. As they approached the lake, they saw a strange figure rise up from the depths of the water. It was humanoid in shape, but its body was twisted and distorted, with elongated limbs and clawed fingers.

The figure let out a piercing scream, sending chills down the spines of the friends. They tried to run, but the figure was too fast, and it began to chase them through the woods.

One by one, the friends were caught by the creature, its sharp claws ripping into their flesh. As they screamed in agony, they saw the creature absorb their life force, their energy draining away as they were consumed by the monster.

The last remaining friend managed to escape, running through the woods in a blind panic. But the creature was relentless, pursuing her until she was cornered at the edge of a cliff. With nowhere left to run, the friend jumped off the cliff, plummeting to her death in the waters below. As she sank to the bottom of the lake, she saw the figure rise up from the depths once more, its glowing eyes fixed on her lifeless body.

The friends were never seen again, and the lake became known as a cursed place, a warning to anyone who dared to venture into the wilderness alone.

# Twisted Apprentice

In a small village nestled in the heart of a dark forest, there lived a young girl named Eliza. She was a curious child, always eager to explore the woods beyond her village, despite the warnings of the elders.

One day, as she wandered deeper into the forest than ever before, she stumbled upon an ancient, crumbling castle. Drawn by her curiosity, she pushed open the doors and stepped inside. As she explored the dark and dusty corridors, she noticed something strange about the castle. The walls seemed to be alive, pulsating with a sickly, green light. Eliza shuddered as she realized that she had stumbled upon the lair of a powerful sorcerer.

She tried to flee, but it was too late. The sorcerer had sensed her presence and appeared before her, his eyes burning with an otherworldly fire. He offered her a deal: he would teach her the secrets of dark magic, but in exchange, she must become his apprentice and serve him for all eternity.

Eliza refused, but the sorcerer was not one to be denied. He cursed her, twisting her body and mind into a twisted, monstrous creature. With no other choice, Eliza pledged herself to the sorcerer, becoming his loyal servant for all eternity. But as she served him, she plotted her revenge, waiting for the day when she could break the sorcerer's hold on her and reclaim her humanity.

Years passed, and Eliza grew more powerful with each passing day. And then, one fateful night, she seized her chance. Using her dark magic, she broke free from the sorcerer's control and turned on him, banishing him to the abyss from which he had come.

With the sorcerer defeated, Eliza was free to explore the world once more, but she knew that the scars of her dark past would always haunt her. She vowed to use her powers for good, to help those in need and to fight against the darkness that threatened to consume her world.

# Laughs to the Grave House

In a small town, a group of friends gathered at the local haunted house on Halloween night, eager to scare each other with spooky stories and pranks. They were a rowdy bunch, always looking for a laugh, and they had no idea what was in store for them that night.

As they settled in for the night, they began telling ghost stories, each one trying to outdo the last. But one of them, a jokester named Jimmy, decided to take things to the next level.

He began to tell a story about a haunted bowling alley, where the ghost of a legendary bowler still haunted the lanes, seeking revenge on anyone who dared to challenge him.

At first, the group laughed and joked, but then something strange began to happen. The lights flickered, and the air grew cold. Suddenly, the group found themselves transported to the haunted bowling alley, facing off against the ghostly bowler. At first, they were terrified, but then they realized that the ghostly bowler was anything but scary.

He was a bumbling, comical figure, always tripping over his own feet and sending bowling balls flying in all directions. The group couldn't help but laugh as they watched the ghostly bowler stumble and fumble his way around the alley, trying and failing to hit a strike. And then, suddenly, he vanished, leaving the group back in the haunted house, their laughter echoing through the halls.

As they looked around, they realized that the haunted house was no longer haunted. The ghosts and ghouls that had once haunted its halls had been banished by their laughter, and the group had unwittingly saved the town from its curse.

From that day forward, the group was known as the "Ghostbusters of laughter," and they continued to tell scary stories and pull pranks, knowing that their laughter was the greatest weapon against the forces of darkness.

# Feathered Fate of Ravenwood

In the small town of Ravenwood, a young detective named Olivia was investigating a series of mysterious disappearances that had been occurring over the past few months. Each time someone went missing, a single black feather was left behind as a clue.

Despite her best efforts, Olivia couldn't seem to find any leads. The townsfolk were tight-lipped, and the more she dug, the more she felt like someone was watching her every move.

One night, as she was walking through the dark woods outside of town, she saw a figure in the distance. It was a tall, shadowy figure, its form indistinct in the gloom. Olivia approached cautiously, her hand on her revolver.

As she drew closer, the figure stepped forward, revealing itself to be a man with a bird's head. He introduced himself as the Raven, the spirit of the woods, and claimed to know the truth about the disappearances.

Olivia was sceptical, but the Raven led her deep into the woods, to a hidden glade where an ancient ritual was being performed. The townsfolk had been sacrificing people to the Raven, hoping to appease the vengeful spirit and protect their town from harm.

Olivia was horrified, but she knew she had to act fast. She confronted the townsfolk and managed to stop the ritual before anyone else could be hurt.

In the end, Olivia was hailed as a hero, and the Raven disappeared back into the woods, his power broken by the revelation of his true nature. But Olivia knew that the memory of the Raven and the sacrifices made in his name would haunt her for the rest of her days.

# A Story of False Paradise

*"In the year 2100, humanity had finally achieved a state of utopia."*

Disease had been eradicated, hunger was a thing of the past, and the world was at peace. The government had created a perfect society where everyone lived in harmony and there was no crime or poverty. But as the years went by, strange things began to happen.

Plants withered and died for no apparent reason, and the sky took on an ominous, blood-red hue. People began to get sick, and no one could figure out why? A group of scientists were brought in to investigate, and what they discovered was horrifying. The utopia that they had worked so hard to create was actually a façade, covering up a dark secret.

The scientists had been experimenting with a new form of genetic engineering, creating a new breed of humans that could survive in the harsh, post-apocalyptic world that they believed was coming. But something had gone terribly wrong. The genetically engineered humans had become a virus, spreading throughout the world and consuming everything in their path.

The utopian society that had once been a beacon of hope was now a breeding ground for a new species of monster. The scientists knew that they had to act fast if they were going to stop the virus from spreading. They created a team of elite soldiers, each one equipped with the latest in high-tech weaponry and biohazard suits.

The team was sent out into the world to fight the virus, but they soon realized that they were facing an enemy unlike any they had ever encountered. The genetically engineered humans were powerful and intelligent, and they seemed to be adapting to their attacks.

The soldiers fought valiantly, but in the end, they were no match for the virus. The world fell into chaos, and the utopian society was destroyed.

In the years that followed, humanity was forced to live in small, isolated communities, constantly on the move to avoid the virus. The world had become a wasteland, with only a few pockets of humanity left. But the memory of the utopia that had been lost, and the horror that had caused its downfall, would haunt them for generations to come.

And as the survivors struggled to survive, they couldn't help but wonder if they would ever be able to create a new utopia, or if their fate was already sealed.

The government had lied to them, and they had paid the ultimate price. The only hope left was to learn from their mistakes and never let something like this happen again.

# Suspense & Thriller

# The Unseen Threat

## Chapter 1

Emma had always been a sceptic of the supernatural, but that changed the night she saw something she couldn't explain. It was a dark figure lurking in the shadows, watching her every move.

She tried to dismiss it as her imagination, but it lingered in the back of her mind. As she walked home, she couldn't shake the feeling that she was being followed.

The next day, Emma's best friend Lily went missing. The police were sceptical of Emma's claims that something supernatural was behind it. They suspected Lily had run away, but Emma knew there was more to the story. She started her own investigation, determined to uncover the truth.

As Emma delved deeper into the case, she began to uncover a web of lies and deceit. Everyone she thought she could trust had a secret to hide.

She started receiving anonymous messages warning her to stop her investigation, but she refused to give up.

# Chapter 2

The more Emma investigated, the more she realized that Lily's disappearance was just the tip of the iceberg. There was a dark force at work in their town, and it was up to her to stop it.

She teamed up with a group of unlikely allies, each with their own reasons for wanting to take down the unseen threat.

The closer they got to the truth, the more dangerous their journey became. They were constantly on the run from those who wanted to silence them. Emma's life was in constant danger, but she refused to back down. She knew that the fate of her town depended on her success.

As Emma and her allies raced towards the final showdown, they uncovered the truth behind the unseen threat. It was a force more powerful than anything they could have ever imagined, and they were the only ones who could stop it.

# Chapter 3

The battle was intense, with losses on both sides, but in the end, they emerged victorious. With the unseen threat defeated, Emma's life slowly returned to normal. She realized that sometimes the things we can't explain are the most real of all. She knew that she would never be the same again, but she was grateful for the experience. It had taught her to trust in the unknown and to never give up, no matter how impossible the odds may seem.

Epilogue Years later, Emma was a successful journalist, always seeking out the truth in every story. She never forgot the lessons she had learned during her investigation of the unseen threat. She continued to believe in the impossible and to fight for what was right, no matter the cost.

# Maggie Forgotten City

## Chapter 1

Maggie had always been fascinated by the stories her grandmother told her about the forgotten city. The city was said to be located deep in the mountains, hidden away from the rest of the world. It was a place of magic and wonder, filled with treasures beyond imagination.

*As a child, Maggie dreamed of one day finding the city and uncovering its secrets.*

Years passed, and Maggie grew up, but her fascination with the forgotten city never faded. She became an archaeologist, studying ancient civilizations and lost cities.

One day, while on a research expedition in the mountains, she stumbled upon a map that she recognized. It was a map of the forgotten city.

Maggie knew that this was her chance to finally find the city she had always dreamed of. She gathered a team of fellow archaeologists and set out on a journey to uncover the secrets of the forgotten city.

They travelled deep into the mountains, facing treacherous terrain and dangerous wildlife along the way.

## **Chapter 2**

As they drew closer to the city, Maggie and her team encountered strange occurrences. They heard whispers on the wind, and felt a presence watching them from the shadows.

But Maggie refused to let her fear stop her from finding the city she had spent her whole life searching for.

Finally, they reached the entrance to the forgotten city. It was unlike anything Maggie had ever seen. The walls were made of shimmering crystal, and the gates were adorned with intricate carvings depicting scenes of ancient battles and great triumphs.

They entered the city, and were immediately struck by the beauty of the architecture and the vastness of the city. As they explored the city, they uncovered more and more secrets.

# **Chapter 3**

They found ancient artifacts and texts that had been lost to time. But they also discovered that the city was not as deserted as they had initially thought. They encountered beings that they could not explain, and strange occurrences that they could not ignore.

The team split up to investigate different parts of the city. Maggie, along with her colleague Adam, stumbled upon a chamber that seemed to be the heart of the city.

It was filled with ancient machinery and technology that they could not comprehend. But as they explored further, they realized that there was something else in the chamber with them. Suddenly, they were attacked by creatures unlike anything they had ever seen. They fought back, but were outnumbered and outmatched.

Just when all seemed lost, they were saved by an unlikely ally. It was a being that had been watching them since they entered the city. It revealed that it was the last remaining inhabitant of the forgotten city, and it needed their help.

# **<u>Chapter 4</u>**

The being explained that the city had been built by an ancient race of beings who had long since gone extinct. They had created the city as a means of harnessing and controlling a great power that had threatened to destroy the world. But in doing so, they had also created a great danger.

The power had become too much for them to control, and it threatened to destroy the world they had sought to save.

The being revealed that it had been left behind to keep the power contained, but it was slowly losing its hold on it. It needed Maggie and her team to help it reseal the power before it was too late.

The team agreed, and they worked together to reseal the power. With the power contained once again, the forgotten city began to crumble. Maggie and her team raced to escape, but they were not fast enough. They were trapped.

# The Lost Heir

## <u>Chapter 1</u>

Princess Isabella had always known that she was different. She had a gift that no one else in the kingdom possessed – the ability to communicate with animals. But she had kept her gift hidden, fearing that her father, the king, would see it as a weakness.

One day, while exploring the woods outside the palace, Isabella stumbled upon a wounded wolf. She used her gift to heal the wolf, and in return, the wolf pledged to protect her.

Isabella was overjoyed to have a friend who understood her gift. But her happiness was short-lived. A few days later, the kingdom was attacked by a neighbouring kingdom. Isabella's father, the king, was killed in battle, and the kingdom was thrown into chaos.

The queen, Isabella's mother, was forced to flee with her daughter and a small group of loyal soldiers. As they fled into the wilderness, Isabella realized that she had been right to keep her gift hidden.

# Chapter 2

The soldiers were sceptical of her abilities, and some even saw her as a liability. But Isabella refused to let her gift go to waste. She used her ability to communicate with animals to help them survive in the wilderness.

They travelled for weeks, with no end in sight. They were running low on supplies, and morale was low. But then they stumbled upon a hidden village deep in the forest.

The villagers welcomed them with open arms, and Isabella felt a glimmer of hope. But that hope was short-lived. The neighbouring kingdom had heard rumours of the hidden village, and they launched an attack. The villagers were outnumbered and outmatched, and Isabella and her mother were forced to flee once again.

# Chapter 3

As they travelled, Isabella began to realize that there was more to her gift than she had originally thought. She could sense that something was not right in the kingdom. It was as if there was a darkness that was slowly taking hold.

Isabella and her mother finally arrived at a castle that was once home to a powerful wizard. The castle was abandoned, but Isabella sensed that there was still magic within its walls. She explored the castle, and eventually stumbled upon a hidden room.

In the room, Isabella discovered a book that contained the secrets of the kingdom. She learned that her father had not died in battle, but had been murdered by a member of his own court. That person had then taken the throne and was using dark magic to control the kingdom.

## **<u>Chapter 4</u>**

Isabella knew that it was up to her to stop the dark magic and restore the rightful heir to the throne. With the help of her animal friends and a small group of loyal soldiers, she set out to confront the usurper.

They battled their way through the castle, facing off against the usurper's minions. Isabella used her gift to call upon the animals of the kingdom, and they rallied to her side. Together, they confronted the usurper.

In a fierce battle, Isabella and the usurper faced off. The usurper was powerful, but Isabella was determined. With the help of her animal friends, she was able to weaken the usurper's hold on the kingdom.

## Chapter 5

Finally, the usurper was defeated, and the true heir to the throne was restored. Isabella was hailed as a hero, and her gift was celebrated. She had proved that her gift was not a weakness, but a strength.

*"As Isabella settled into her new."*

# Silent Will be Witness

## Chapter 1

The sound of rain tapping against the windowpane filled the room as Detective Mark Austin sat at his desk, staring at the case file in front of him. He had been working on the case for weeks, but it felt like he was no closer to finding the killer.

The latest victim, a young woman named Sarah, had been found dead in her apartment. Her body had been brutally beaten and left in a pool of blood. The killer had left no clues, no witnesses, and no traceable evidence.

Mark had been going over the evidence repeatedly, trying to piece together the killer's motive and identity. He had no leads, but he knew he had to keep digging. He flipped through the pages of the file again, trying to find something that he might have missed.

Suddenly, there was a knock on his door. Mark looked up to see his partner, Detective Sarah Thompson, standing in the doorway.

"Mark, we got a lead," she said, handing him a piece of paper.

Mark took the paper and read the address on it. "This is the address of the witness who found Sarah's body," he said, looking up at Sarah.

"Why didn't we interview him before?"

"We did, but he didn't have anything useful to tell us," Sarah said.

"But he just called the station, said he had some new information about the case. I think we should go and talk to him again."

Mark nodded and grabbed his coat.

"Let's go."

The two detectives drove to the witness's address and parked their car outside.

The witness, a middle-aged man named John, greeted them at the door.

"Come in, come in," he said, ushering them into his living room.

## **Chapter 2**

Mark and Sarah sat down on the sofa as John poured them each a cup of coffee. He then sat down opposite them and took a sip of his own coffee.

"I'm sorry to bother you again," Mark said, "but we appreciate any information you can give us."

John nodded. "I didn't tell you everything last time," he said. "I was scared. But I think I know who did it."

Mark and Sarah leaned forward; their attention fully focused on John.

"I heard something that night," John said. "I live next door to Sarah's apartment, and I heard a commotion.

I went out to the hallway and saw a man leaving her apartment. He was tall, muscular, and had a scar on his left cheek."

*"Did you recognize him?" Sarah asked.*

"No, I didn't," John said. "But I remembered seeing him around the neighbourhood. He looked like a construction worker."

Mark jotted down the information in his notepad. "Thank you for telling us this, John," he said. "We'll look into it." As they left John's apartment, Mark's mind raced with possibilities.

He knew they had to find this construction worker with a scar on his cheek. He and Sarah went back to the station and started going through the list of construction workers in the area.

Days turned into weeks, and Mark and Sarah worked tirelessly to find the killer. They interviewed dozens of construction workers, but none of them matched the description given by John.

Mark was starting to lose hope, but he knew he couldn't give up. One night, Mark was sitting alone in his office when he received a call from Sarah.

"Mark, you need to come to the crime scene right now," she said, her voice trembling.

"What happened?" Mark asked, his heart racing.

"We found another victim," Sarah said. "It's the witness, John." Mark rushed to the crime scene, his mind racing with questions.

## **Chapter 3**

Mark arrived at the crime scene to find a crowd of police officers and detectives gathered outside John's apartment building. Sarah was waiting for him at the entrance.

"Are you okay?" Mark asked, looking at her worriedly.

"I'm fine," Sarah said, her voice barely above a whisper. "But it's John. He's dead, Mark. He was killed in the same way as Sarah."

Mark's heart sank as he pushed past the crowd and entered the apartment. John's body was lying in the living room, his face twisted in agony.

Mark felt a wave of anger and frustration wash over him. They had failed to protect the witness, and now another innocent person was dead.

Mark and Sarah worked tirelessly to find any new leads, but it seemed like they had hit a dead end. They went over the evidence again and again, trying to find something that they had missed.

It was then that Mark noticed something strange about the crime scene photos. John's body was lying in a different position than the first victim's body.

"Sarah, look at this," Mark said, pointing to the photo.

"John's body is facing a different direction than Sarah's body."

Sarah looked at the photo and then back at Mark, a glimmer of hope in her eyes.

"That means there could have been another person in the apartment,"

she spoke. "Someone who moved John's body."

Mark nodded. "We need to find that person," he said. "We need to find the real killer."

## **<u>Chapter 4</u>**

They went back to the witness list and started going through it again. It was then that they found a name that they had overlooked before. It was a construction worker named Jack, who had a scar on his left cheek.

Mark and Sarah tracked down Jack and brought him in for questioning. At first, he denied any involvement in the murders, but as they presented him with more and more evidence, he started to crack. He confessed to killing both Sarah and John.

*"I didn't mean to kill them,"* Jack said, tears streaming down his face. "It was an accident.

I just wanted to rob them, but they fought back. I didn't know what else to do."

Mark and Sarah arrested Jack and took him to trial. He was found guilty of both murders and sentenced to life in prison.

Mark and Sarah sat in the courtroom; their eyes fixed on Jack as he was led away in handcuffs.

They had finally found justice for the victims, but they knew that the memory of the case would haunt them forever.

As they left the courthouse, Sarah turned to Mark and said, "I don't think I could have solved this case without you, Mark."

Mark smiled. "I couldn't have done it without you either, Sarah,"

He spoke. "We make a good team."

And with that, they walked out of the courthouse, ready to face whatever new case came their way.

# Chapter 5

Mark and Sarah continued to work together, solving more cases and bringing criminals to justice. They formed a close bond, both personally and professionally, and their partnership was highly respected in the department.

Years went by, and they both rose through the ranks, becoming highly decorated detectives. They never forgot about Sarah and John, and the impact their murders had on them. But they took solace in the fact that they were able to find justice for them and their families. As they looked back on their careers, they realized that they had made a difference in the world, no matter how small.

They had protected the innocent, and they had fought against those who sought to do harm. And as they retired from the force, they knew that they had left the world a little bit better than they found it.

# Unseen Observer

## Chapter 1

After solving the case of the serial killer who had murdered Sarah and John, Mark and Sarah were approached by a wealthy businessman named Robert.

Robert had a unique proposition for them. He wanted them to investigate a series of bizarre deaths that had occurred at his company's research facility.

Mark and Sarah were hesitant at first, but the offer was too good to pass up. Robert promised them a generous pay out, as well as access to state-of-the-art equipment and resources. As they delved deeper into the case, they realized that something sinister was going on at the research facility.

They discovered that the company had been experimenting on human subjects, using them to develop new drugs and technologies.

Mark and Sarah were horrified by what they had uncovered, but they knew that they had to keep digging. They knew that they had stumbled upon something bigger than themselves, something that could change the world as they knew it. As they got closer to the truth, they found themselves being targeted by the company's hired guns. They were constantly on the run, trying to stay one step ahead of their pursuers.

Finally, they discovered the truth. Robert, the man who had hired them, was the mastermind behind the experiments. He had been using the subjects as guinea pigs, testing out new drugs and technologies without any regard for their safety or well-being. But Robert was just a small piece of a larger puzzle.

Mark and Sarah had uncovered a shadow organization that had been operating in secret, pulling the strings behind some of the world's most powerful corporations and governments.

## **Chapter 2**

The organization knew that Mark and Sarah had uncovered their secret, and they were not going to let them live. Mark and Sarah were in a race against time to stop the organization before they could carry out their plans.

In a final showdown, Mark and Sarah faced off against the leaders of the organization. It was a brutal and bloody battle, but in the end, Mark and Sarah emerged victorious. As they looked out over the smouldering ruins of the organization's headquarters,

Mark turned to Sarah and said, "I never imagined that we would be fighting against something like this."

Sarah nodded, her eyes wide with disbelief.

"I know," she said. "But we did it. We saved the world from a group of power-hungry madmen."

Mark smiled, feeling a sense of accomplishment wash over him. "We make a pretty good team," he said. And with that, they walked off into the sunset, ready for whatever new challenges lay ahead.

# Past of Mark and Sarah

## <u>Chapter 1</u>

**M**ark and Sarah thought that they had seen it all. They had fought against serial killers, corrupt politicians, and shadowy organizations. But as they retired from the police force and settled into their new lives, they soon realized that there were new challenges on the horizon.

It all started with a phone call. Sarah picked up the phone, expecting to hear from a telemarketer or someone trying to sell her something. But the voice on the other end was one that she recognized all too well.

"Sarah," the voice said. "It's Robert. I need your help."

Sarah's heart sank. She had thought that she had put Robert and his twisted experiments behind her. But apparently, he wasn't finished with her yet.

"What do you want, Robert?" she asked, trying to keep her voice steady.

"I need you and Mark to come to my office," Robert said. "I have a proposition for you."

Sarah hesitated. She didn't want to get involved with Robert again. But something in his voice made her curious.

"Fine," she said. "We'll come to your office. But we're not making any promises." As they drove to Robert's office, Sarah and Mark couldn't help but feel uneasy.

They had a bad feeling about this. When they arrived at the office, they were met by Robert and his assistant, a young woman named Emily.

"Thank you for coming," Robert said, gesturing for them to sit down.

"I know that you're probably still angry with me for what I did in the past. But I need your help."

Sarah and Mark exchanged a sceptical glance. "What kind of help?" Mark asked.

## **Chapter 2**

Robert leaned forward; his eyes intense. "I need you to help me stop a group of terrorists."

Sarah and Mark sat up straight, suddenly alert. "Terrorists?" Sarah asked.

Robert nodded. "Yes. They're planning to launch an attack on the city. And I know that you two are the only ones who can stop them."

Sarah and Mark were hesitant. They didn't trust Robert, and they weren't sure that they wanted to get involved in something like this. But they also knew that they had a duty to protect the people of the city.

"Fine," Sarah said, sighing.

"We'll help you. But you're going to have to be completely transparent with us."

Robert nodded. "Of course. I'll tell you everything that I know."

Over the next few days, Sarah and Mark worked tirelessly, gathering information about the terrorist group and their plans. They scoured the city, talking to informants and trying to piece together the puzzle.

As they got closer to the truth, they realized that the situation was far more complicated than they had initially thought. The terrorist group was just a small piece of a larger puzzle, and they were being manipulated by a shadowy organization that had infiltrated every level of society.

Sarah and Mark were shocked by what they had uncovered. They had always known that there were dark forces at work in the world, but they had never imagined that they were this powerful. But they didn't have time to dwell on their shock.

They had a job to do. They had to stop the terrorist group before they could carry out their plans. In a tense standoff, Sarah and Mark faced off against the terrorist group. It was a brutal and bloody battle, but in the end, they emerged victorious. But their victory was short-lived. As they were celebrating their success, they received a phone call from Robert.

## **Chapter 3**

"I'm sorry," Robert said, his voice shaking. "But I had to do it. I had to betray you."

Sarah and Mark were stunned. "What are you talking about?" Sarah asked.

Robert took a deep breath before speaking. "The truth is, the terrorist group that you just defeated was just a distraction.

The real threat was something much bigger."

Sarah and Mark felt their hearts drop as they realized what Robert was saying.

"What is it?" Mark asked, trying to keep his voice steady.

"The shadowy organization that I told you about," Robert said.

"They're planning to launch a massive attack on the city. They're going to use a new weapon that they've developed, something that will cause widespread destruction and chaos." Sarah and Mark felt a chill run down their spines.

They had to act fast. "Where is this weapon?" Sarah asked. "It's being transported to the city right now," Robert said. "I don't know where it is, but I do know that it's going to be here within the next 24 hours."

## **<u>Chapter 4</u>**

Sarah and Mark didn't waste any time. They worked with Robert to gather as much information as they could about the shadowy organization and their plans.

They knew that they were facing an impossible task, but they were determined to do everything in their power to stop the attack.

As they raced against the clock, Sarah and Mark uncovered a shocking truth: the shadowy organization was being funded by a wealthy businessman who had his sights set on world domination. With this new information, Sarah and Mark knew that they couldn't just stop the attack on the city. They had to take down the entire organization.

In a desperate and dangerous mission, Sarah and Mark infiltrated the organization's headquarters.

It was a dangerous and deadly journey, but they were able to destroy the weapon and take down the organization. As they emerged from the smouldering ruins of the headquarters, Sarah and Mark felt a sense of relief wash over them.

They had done it. They had saved the city, and maybe even the world. But their victory was bittersweet. They had faced unimaginable challenges, and they knew that there were more waiting for them in the future. But they were ready for whatever lay ahead. They had each other, and that was all that mattered.

# The Detective and Deceit

## Chapter 1

John was one of the best detectives in the city. He had solved some of the most complex cases in record time, and his reputation preceded him wherever he went. But even he was stumped by the recent bank heist that had taken place in the city. The heist had been meticulously planned, with the robbers using advanced technology to bypass the bank's security systems. They had made off with millions of dollars, leaving no trace behind.

John had been assigned to the case, and he had been working tirelessly to gather evidence and piece together what had happened. But despite his best efforts, he was still no closer to solving the case.

One day, as John was pouring over the surveillance footage from the bank, something caught his eye. A man had walked into the bank just minutes before the heist had taken place, and he had left just as quickly.

John's instincts told him that this man was somehow involved in the heist, and he immediately set out to track him down. He combed through the footage, trying to get a better look at the man's face, but he couldn't make out any features. It was like the man had deliberately disguised himself.

John spent the next few days following every lead he could find, but nothing seemed to lead him any closer to the man he was looking for. Then, he received a call from an anonymous source.

"I know who you're looking for," the voice on the other end of the line said.

"Meet me at the old warehouse on Main Street tonight at midnight."

John didn't know if he could trust the voice on the other end of the line, but he didn't have any other leads.

He made his way to the warehouse, his gun at the ready. As he entered the warehouse, he saw a man standing in the shadows.

"I've been expecting you," the man said, stepping forward. It was the same man from the surveillance footage.

He had a sly smile on his face as he looked at John. "You're involved in the heist, aren't you?" John said, his gun trained on the man.

The man chuckled. "I suppose you could say that," he said. "But it's not what you think. I didn't steal anything."

John was confused. "Then what are you doing here?"

## Chapter 2

The man sighed. "I was hired to create a distraction," he said. "The people who robbed the bank needed a way to get in and out without being detected. So, I caused a commotion outside the bank to distract the guards."

John was shocked. "Who hired you?" he asked.

The man hesitated.

"I can't tell you that, "he said.

"But I can tell you that they're planning another heist, and it's going to be even bigger than the last one."

John realized that he had stumbled onto something much bigger than he had originally thought. He knew that he had to act fast to stop the next heist from taking place.

Over the next few days, John pieced together more and more information about the heist. He discovered that the robbers were planning to hit another bank in the city, and they were going to use a similar distraction to get in and out undetected.

But John had an idea. He knew that the robbers were going to use a high-frequency sound device to create the distraction. He also knew that this device would only work on humans.

So, he recruited a team of trained dogs to guard the bank. The dogs were immune to the high-frequency sound and would be able to alert the guards if anything suspicious was happening.

The day of the heist arrived, and John watched as the robbers tried to carry out their plan. But the dogs did their job, and the

# **Chapter 3**

Robbers were caught in the act. John and his team swooped in and arrested the entire group. But the puzzle wasn't solved yet. John wanted to know who was behind the heist, who had hired the robbers in the first place.

He dug deeper, looking for any clues he could find. It was then that he came across a name - Samuel Wilson. Wilson was a wealthy businessman who owned several companies in the city. John suspected that he was the mastermind behind the heist.

He spent the next few days gathering evidence and building a case against Wilson. He was confident that he had enough to take him down. But as he was about to make his move, he received a call from Wilson himself.

"I know what you're up to," Wilson said. "But you'll never be able to prove anything."

John was taken aback. "What are you talking about?" he asked.

Wilson chuckled.

"You think you're so smart," he said. "But you've overlooked one crucial detail."

John didn't know what he was talking about.

"You see," Wilson continued, "I didn't actually steal anything. The money was never mine to begin with."

John was confused. "What are you saying?"

Wilson sighed. "The bank was laundering money for one of my companies," he said. "I simply took back what was rightfully mine."

John couldn't believe what he was hearing. "That doesn't justify stealing millions of dollars," he said.

"Maybe not," Wilson replied. "But it's not like the bank was going to give it back willingly."

John was at a loss for words. He had never encountered a case like this before.

Wilson was technically right - the money wasn't stolen if it belonged to him to begin with. But it still didn't sit right with John.

In the end, Wilson wasn't charged with anything. He had found a loophole in the system, and there was nothing John could do about it. But the case had opened John's eyes to the complexities of the justice system.

It wasn't always as black and white as he had thought. Sometimes, there were shades of grey that made it difficult to see the truth. As he walked out of the courthouse, John knew that he would never forget the bank heist and the challenges it had presented. It had changed him in ways he couldn't even begin to imagine.

## **Chapter 4**

Despite the outcome of the case, John couldn't shake the feeling that there was more to the story. He continued to investigate, trying to find any other links or clues that might help him understand what had really happened.

One day, he received a call from an anonymous source. The person claimed to have information about the bank heist and was willing to meet with John to discuss it further.

John was intrigued and arranged to meet the person in a secluded area outside the city. When he arrived, he found a man waiting for him. The man was nervous and jumpy, clearly afraid of being caught.

He handed John a file and whispered, "You need to see this. It will explain everything."

John took the file and thanked the man. As he began to read through it, he realized that it contained evidence that connected Samuel Wilson to a larger criminal organization.

It seemed that Wilson had been using the bank to launder money for the organization, and the bank heist was just one small part of a larger plan to take control of the city's criminal underworld.

John knew that he had to act fast. He contacted his team and began to plan a raid on Wilson's companies. They worked tirelessly, gathering evidence and building a case against Wilson and his associates.

Finally, the day of the raid arrived. John and his team stormed into Wilson's offices and began to make arrests. Wilson tried to flee, but he was quickly apprehended.

In the end, Wilson and his associates were charged with multiple counts of money laundering, extortion, and conspiracy. The evidence that John had gathered had been enough to build a solid case against them, and they were all sentenced to long prison terms.

As John walked out of the courthouse, he couldn't help but feel a sense of satisfaction. The bank heist had led him down a path that he never would have imagined, but in the end, it had all been worth it.

The case had taught him that sometimes, the truth was hidden behind layers of complexity and deceit. But if he was willing to dig deep and follow the clues, he could uncover even the most well-hidden secrets. And that was a challenge that he was more than willing to take on.

## **Chapter 5**

Despite the successful conclusion of the bank heist investigation, John couldn't help but feel like there was still more work to be done. He knew that there were still criminals out there who were operating under the radar, and he was determined to bring them to justice.

Over the next few months, John and his team focused on investigating other criminal organizations in the city. They worked tirelessly, gathering evidence and building cases against those who were breaking the law. It wasn't easy - many of the criminals they were targeting were smart and cunning, and they knew how to stay hidden from the authorities. But John was relentless, and he refused to give up until justice had been served.

Slowly but surely, John began to make progress. He and his team were able to bust several major criminal operations, taking down drug rings, smuggling rings, and more.

The people of the city began to take notice. John had become something of a local hero, and people looked up to him as someone who was willing to stand up to the criminals who were wreaking havoc on their city. But John knew that the work was never truly done.

For every criminal organization that he took down, there were ten more waiting in the wings, ready to take their place.

He continued to work tirelessly, always on the lookout for the next big case. And as he did, he began to realize that there was more to life than just fighting crime. He had been so consumed with his work that he had forgotten about the other things that mattered - his family, his friends, his hobbies.

It was then that he made a decision. He would continue to fight crime, but he would also make time for the other things that mattered in life. He would spend more time with his family, take up new hobbies, and try to find a balance between his work and his personal life.

## **Chapter 6**

And so, John continued to work as a detective, always on the lookout for the next big challenge. But he also took time to enjoy the simple things in life - a walk in the park, a good book, a meal with his loved ones.

He knew that the challenges of life would always be there, but he was ready to face them head-on, armed with the knowledge and experience that he had gained over the years. And as he looked out over the city, he couldn't help but feel a sense of satisfaction.

He had come a long way from the rookie detective who had first walked into the precinct so many years ago. But he knew that there was still much more work to be done, and he was ready for whatever lay ahead.

# The Bangkok Heist

## <u>Chapter 1</u>

*"It was a humid afternoon in the bustling city of Bangkok, Thailand."*

The sun was beating down mercilessly, and the streets were crowded with people going about their daily business. But in a small financial institution on the outskirts of the city, something sinister was afoot.

A group of masked men had stormed into the bank, wielding guns and shouting orders. They quickly took control of the situation, forcing the terrified employees and customers to lie down on the ground.

The robbers went straight for the vault, which held millions of baht in cash and valuable assets. They knew exactly what they were doing - they had clearly planned this heist for months, maybe even years.

The police were called, but by the time they arrived, the robbers had already fled the scene, leaving behind a trail of destruction and fear.

Detective Aroon, a seasoned investigator with the Royal Thai Police, was assigned to the case. He knew that the investigation wouldn't be easy - the robbers had left very few clues, and the bank's security cameras had been disabled.

Aroon knew that he needed to think outside the box if he was going to crack this case. He began to dig deep into the cultural and social aspects of the city, trying to find any information that could lead to a breakthrough.

He soon discovered that the heist had been executed by a group of criminals who were well-versed in the cultural nuances of Thailand. They had used traditional Thai masks as a disguise, and their communication was done using code words and phrases that only locals would understand.

## **Chapter 2**

Aroon also found out that the robbers had hidden the stolen money and assets in different parts of the city, using a complex puzzle-like system that only they could decipher.

Determined to catch the criminals and recover the stolen goods, Aroon enlisted the help of a young woman named Nisa. Nisa was a graduate student in cryptography, and her expertise in puzzles and codes proved to be invaluable.

Together, Aroon and Nisa began to piece together the clues, using their combined knowledge of Thai culture and puzzles to unravel the mystery. As they delved deeper into the case, they discovered that the heist had been masterminded by a wealthy businessman who had ties to organized crime.

The businessman had used his knowledge of Thai culture to recruit a group of expert criminals, promising them a share of the loot in exchange for their help. With this new information, Aroon and Nisa were able to track down the criminals and recover the stolen goods. They also arrested the businessman, who was later charged and convicted for his role in the heist. As the case came to a close, Aroon couldn't help but feel a sense of pride in his country and its rich cultural heritage.

He knew that the robbers had tried to use that culture against them, but in the end, it was that very same culture that had helped them crack the case. And as he walked out of the bank, with the sound of police sirens ringing in his ears, Aroon couldn't help but feel grateful for the unexpected ally he had found in Nisa, and for the unique mix of culture and puzzle-solving skills that had helped them solve the case.

# Chapter 3

After the successful recovery of the stolen goods and the arrest of the mastermind behind the heist, Detective Aroon and Nisa thought their work was done. But they soon realized that there was more to the case than they had initially thought.

As they dug deeper into the evidence, they found a number of discrepancies that didn't add up. The more they investigated, the more they realized that there were still unanswered questions about the heist.

They discovered that the businessman they had arrested wasn't the true mastermind behind the heist. He was just a pawn, taking orders from someone else who was still out there, lurking in the shadows.

Aroon and Nisa knew that they had to find out who this person was, and fast. They feared that another heist was already in the works, and they didn't want to see innocent people hurt again.

With renewed determination, they began to piece together the remaining clues, trying to find the missing piece of the puzzle.

Their investigation took them to the heart of Bangkok's criminal underworld, where they met with a group of high-level informants who promised to help them find the true mastermind.

It wasn't long before they got a break in the case. One of the informants told them about a secret meeting that was going to take place in a secluded location on the outskirts of the city.

## **Chapter 4**

Aroon and Nisa knew that they had to act fast. They gathered a team of skilled officers, and together they made their way to the location. They arrived just in time to catch the mastermind in the act. He was a wealthy businessman, just like the one they had arrested before, but this one was even more powerful and cunning.

The mastermind had planned another heist, even more audacious than the last one. He had recruited a new team of criminals, and they were about to execute the plan. Aroon and his team swooped in, catching the criminals red-handed.

The mastermind tried to make a run for it, but Aroon chased him down and apprehended him. With the true mastermind behind bars, Aroon and Nisa finally felt a sense of closure. They had solved the case and prevented another heist from taking place. As they walked out of the bank, they knew that their work wasn't over. They had to continue to fight against the criminal underworld and protect the innocent people of Bangkok.

But they also knew that they had each other, and that their unique mix of cultural knowledge and puzzle-solving skills would always be an asset in their fight for justice.

# **Chapter 5**

Aroon and Nisa left the bank, they were greeted by the warm sun shining over the bustling streets of Bangkok. They took a moment to catch their breath and reflect on the events of the past few days.

"I can't believe we actually caught the real mastermind behind the heist," said Nisa, still in disbelief.

Aroon nodded in agreement. "It was a close call, but we did it. And we couldn't have done it without your help, Nisa."

Nisa smiled, feeling a sense of pride and accomplishment.

"Thanks, Aroon. I couldn't have done it without you either. We make a great team."

They both knew that they couldn't rest on their laurels. There would always be more criminals out there, planning their next heist or scam. But for now, they decided to take a well-deserved break and enjoy the sights and sounds of their city. They visited some of their favourite street food vendors and indulged in some delicious Thai cuisine.

As they walked through the city streets, they noticed a sense of unity and community among the people. Despite the recent heist and other criminal activity, the people of Bangkok remained resilient and strong.

Aroon and Nisa realized that this was the true spirit of their city, and they were proud to be a part of it. They were dedicated to protecting their fellow citizens and preserving the culture and traditions that made Bangkok so unique.

Their work wasn't always easy, but they knew that they were making a difference in their community. And for them, that was more than enough. As the sun began to set over the city, Aroon and Nisa said their goodbyes, each headed to their own homes. But they both knew that they would see each other soon, and that they would continue to fight for justice together.

As Aroon entered his apartment, he noticed a note on his kitchen counter. It was from Nisa, thanking him for his partnership and offering to buy him dinner the following week.

Aroon smiled, knowing that their work was far from over. But with Nisa by his side, he was ready to face whatever challenges lay ahead.

# The Puzzle Uncovering Truth

## Chapter 1

The old mansion had been abandoned for years, the once-lavish gardens now overgrown and unkempt.

It was said that the previous owner, a wealthy heiress, had disappeared without a trace, leaving behind a fortune in treasure and an unsolvable mystery. But that didn't stop the four friends from exploring the mansion's labyrinthine corridors and hidden passageways, searching for clues and treasure.

As they searched the dusty old rooms, they stumbled upon a series of cryptic puzzles and riddles, each leading them deeper into the mansion's secrets. The first puzzle was a series of numbers etched into the walls of the grand ballroom.

After hours of trying different combinations, they finally cracked the code, revealing a hidden compartment in the fireplace. Inside, they found a dusty old journal, its pages filled with strange symbols and diagrams. The second puzzle was a riddle carved into the wooden panelling of the library. After much debate and brainstorming, they finally deciphered the clues and discovered a hidden staircase leading to the mansion's subterranean level. As they descended deeper into the mansion's bowels, the puzzles grew more complex and the danger more real.

## **Chapter 2**

They dodged booby traps and solved intricate puzzles, each clue leading them closer to the treasure. But as they approached the final puzzle, they realized that they were not alone in the mansion. Someone was watching them, lurking in the shadows.

Suddenly, the friends found themselves trapped in a room, the door locked and the ceiling slowly descending upon them. Panic set in as they scrambled to solve the final puzzle, each second ticking by like an eternity.

Finally, with moments to spare, they solved the puzzle, revealing the location of the treasure. But as they rushed to claim their prize, they were met with the figure of a hooded stranger, holding a gun.

"You thought you could solve my puzzles and steal my treasure?" the stranger hissed. "Think again."

The friends had been so focused on the puzzles that they had failed to consider the danger that lay ahead. But they refused to give up without a fight. In the ensuing struggle, they managed to disarm the stranger and call the police. The treasure was seized, and the mystery of the heiress's disappearance was finally solved.

As they looked back on their adventure, the friends realized that the real treasure wasn't the wealth they had sought, but the bond they had forged through their shared experiences and challenges.

They knew that they would always have each other, and that no puzzle or mystery could ever break their friendship.

## **Chapter 3**

Years passed since their adventure in the old mansion, but the four friends remained as close as ever. They would often reminisce about their treasure hunt and the challenges they faced along the way.

One day, while they were gathered at a cafe, a stranger approached their table. He was a tall, imposing man with piercing eyes and a deep, gravelly voice.

"I couldn't help but overhear your conversation," he said, gesturing to their animated discussion about the old mansion. "I have a proposition for you."

The friends were wary, but the stranger's offer intrigued them. He claimed to be a collector of rare and exotic artifacts and had a lead on a priceless artifact in a far-off land.

"But," he added, "the artifact is hidden behind a series of complex puzzles and traps. I need a team with your unique set of skills to help me retrieve it."

## **Chapter 4**

The friends looked at each other, a mixture of excitement and trepidation coursing through them. They had sworn off treasure hunting after their last adventure, but the lure of a new puzzle and the promise of adventure proved too strong.

They agreed to the stranger's offer, and he revealed the location of the artifact: a remote temple deep in the heart of a jungle in Southeast Asia.

The journey to the temple was long and treacherous, with the friends facing all manner of challenges along the way. But finally, they arrived at the temple's entrance, a massive stone doorway covered in ancient symbols and markings.

The stranger guided them through the intricate puzzles and traps, each more challenging than the last. The friends worked together, using their unique skills and knowledge to solve the puzzles and move closer to the artifact.

But as they neared the inner sanctum of the temple, they realized that the stranger had a hidden agenda. He wasn't just after the artifact; he was after something else entirely.

It was a race against time as the friends raced to retrieve the artifact and escape the temple before it was too late. They dodged traps and solved puzzles, with each passing second bringing them closer to the truth.

In the end, they emerged victorious, but not without paying a heavy price. The artifact was theirs, but they had uncovered a conspiracy that reached far beyond their adventure in the temple.

As they reflected on their journey, the friends realized that the true puzzle was not the artifact, but the truth behind the stranger's motives. And they knew that they would always be there for each other, no matter what challenges lay ahead.

# Chapter 5

The four friends returned home with the priceless artifact, but they couldn't shake the feeling that something was off. They couldn't just let the stranger's true motives go unchallenged.

So, they dug deeper and uncovered a web of corruption and deceit that stretched far beyond the temple in Southeast Asia.

They worked tirelessly to expose the truth and bring those responsible to justice. It was a long and difficult road, but the friends' unique set of skills and unwavering determination helped them overcome even the toughest challenges.

They solved puzzles, deciphered codes, and outsmarted their opponents at every turn.

In the end, they emerged victorious, with the truth finally exposed and justice served. And as they looked back on their journey, they realized that the real treasure was the bond they shared and the challenges they overcame together.

They vowed to always be there for each other, no matter what new puzzles and adventures lay ahead. And as they set their sights on their next challenge, they knew that they were unstoppable when they worked together as a team.

"Make Sure You
Don't Miss a Thing, *Love* It"
"Make Sure You Don't Miss a
Thing, *Live* It"

# Finally, I Started **W**riting....

**Pugal:** Hey *Yazhini*, I've been thinking about what we should write in our book of short stories. What do you think about exploring themes of love and horror?

*Yazhini:* I like that idea, Pugal. But how can we incorporate humour into these serious themes?

**Pugal:** Well, what if we write a horror story about a couple on a romantic getaway who stumble upon a haunted house? We can add some funny moments to lighten the mood, like the couple arguing over which room to sleep in, with one being convinced it's haunted while the other thinks it's all in their head.

*Yazhini:* That's a great idea! We could also write a love story about a couple who bond over their love of horror movies, but their different preferences on what makes a good scary movie leads to some comical disagreements.

**Pugal:** Yes! We can have one of them love gory slasher films while the other prefers more psychological horror. We could also write about a couple who have a love-hate relationship, where they are constantly bickering and arguing but can't seem to stay away from each other.

*Yazhini:* I like the sound of that. We could also write a horror story where the protagonist is in a love triangle with two supernatural beings, like a vampire and a werewolf, and add some humour to make it more light-hearted.

**Pugal:** That's a good idea, *Yazhini.* We could also write a story about a couple who have to navigate a zombie apocalypse together, with some funny moments thrown in to lighten the mood.

*Yazhini:* Those are all great ideas, Pugal. I think with our combined creativity, we can come up with a collection of short stories that combine love, horror, and humour in a unique and interesting way.

**Pugal:** Agreed, *Yazhini.* I can't wait to start writing and see where our ideas take us.

**Pugal:** You know, *Yazhini,* I was thinking we could also write a horror story that parodies classic horror movie tropes. We could have characters that are aware of the horror movie cliches and try to avoid them, but still end up getting killed off in ridiculous ways.

*Yazhini:* Oh, I like that! We could also have a love story that's set in a post-apocalyptic world, where two survivors fall in love amidst all the chaos and destruction.

**Pugal:** That's a great idea, *Yazhini.* We could add some funny moments by having the characters struggling to find basic necessities like food and water, but still trying to make their relationship work.

*Yazhini:* I also had an idea for a horror story where a group of friends go on a camping trip and accidentally awaken an ancient monster. We could add some humour by having the characters argue over how to defeat the monster, with each one coming up with increasingly ridiculous ideas.

**Pugal:** Ha-ha, I love it! We could also have a love story where the two main characters are ghosts who haunt the same house. They could initially be at odds with each other, but eventually learn to work together and fall in love.

*Yazhini:* That's a really unique idea, Pugal. We could also have a horror story set in a haunted hotel, with the staff trying to hide the ghostly activity from the guests. We could add some humour by having the guests be completely oblivious to the supernatural events happening around them.

**Pugal:** Yes, and we could also write a love story about a couple who are from two different worlds, like a human and an alien. We could add some humour by having them struggle to communicate due to their different languages and cultural differences.

*Yazhini:* Those are all fantastic ideas, Pugal! I think we're onto something here. Let's start writing and see where these stories take us.

*Yazhini:* "*Love and horror* can be a deadly combination, but *adding humour* can make it a delightful read."

**Pugal:** "I couldn't agree more. *Let's get to writing!*"

*******

**Pugal *Yazhini***

*******

**Life** is a **Journey**

## *THE END*

**Love** and **Live**

Milton Keynes UK
Ingram Content Group UK Ltd.
UKHW021053200324
439767UK00015B/464

9 798223 013457